The First Female Navy SEAL

MEGAN HERNANDEZ

C. C. Chamberlane

The First Female Navy SEAL

Megan Hernandez, Volume 3

C. C. Chamberlane

Published by C. C. Chamberlane, 2022.

THE FIRST FEMALE NAVY SEAL

First edition. February 16, 2022.

Copyright © 2022 C. C. Chamberlane.

ISBN: 978-1775373223

Written by C. C. Chamberlane.

Also by C. C. Chamberlane

Megan Hernandez
Samaela
The First Female Navy SEAL
Saving Ukraine

Standalone
Abbadon

Table of Contents

The First Female Navy SEAL – Megan Hernandez

C. C. CHAMBERLANE

Megan Hernandez had always excelled in school, on the field and in life. She was Einstein-smart and professional athlete talented. She was just the type organizations like the FBI and military identified early and watched closely to see if they had what it takes.

This book is about Megan before ABBADON or SAMAELA, when she operated solely on the right side of the law becoming the first female Navy SEAL.

Find out what motivated her to go down the road she did and what really makes her tick.

If you have comments or ideas, please email us directly at CCChamberlane@gmail.com

@ccchamberlane

ISBN Print – 978-1-7753732-2-3
Published by C.C.Chamberlane

Acknowledgements

I am pleased to offer this third novel about Megan Hernandez for your reading pleasure. This book is dedicated to all the loyal fans who have read ABBADON and SAMAELA and I hope you like this one just as much, if not more. Thank you all for your support.

About the Author – C.C. Chamberlane

This is the third fact-influenced-fiction crime novel in a series that features the exploits of Megan Hernandez, the First Female Navy SEAL. I really hope you enjoy this one too! In this prequel to Abbadon, you will learn about Megan's upbringing and education and find out what made her the warrior she is today.

I have always been a true crime type person as these stories are multi-layered and stimulate deep thought. I find both the character development and plot development fascinating and have always been a fan.

Keep an eye on our Facebook page at C.C.Chamberlane and watch for the next title in the series.

Prologue

Megan's Mom: We already had four children, all of them boys, when we found out we were pregnant again. We discovered we were finally having a girl.

I had mixed emotions for a brief time. I had put my successful career on the back burner four times previously to give birth to our wonderful sons. I perhaps got more leeway than other detectives because I could close the toughest cases. I was known at all levels within the police force as, not only did I close a lot of cases, but I was also the lead detective on some high-profile ones.

I'm no idiot, I think it was partially due to my good looks that I was always granted an opportunity to speak about my own cases, once they were solved. I knew that our police department, and most all others, wanted to attract more women into the ranks. I didn't really mind being the poster woman for such a noble cause. I too wanted more women in the ranks as I always knew we could do anything a man could.

I like to think it wasn't only an equity issue but also because women look at things differently than men. Our thought processes move along different paths, and, in some cases, we were better able to analyze motives.

We also typically score higher on the EQ side of testing which can be a benefit to understanding the criminal mind.

I can also still do the job at a very high level, whether I have four children or not. I trained regularly with my husband, Esai, and we were both in top shape. We took physical training as seriously as we did education and continuous learning. We had long ago decided that the best way to stay alive in the occupations we were in was to simply be the best.

I wondered what our daughter would look like. It was very easy to tell our sons belong to Esai, no need for DNA testing there, but this would be our first girl. It was almost laughable how much the boys resembled him at various points in their lives. Thankfully, I could also see sides of me in them as well.

The boys had his rugged good looks and stature. Esai never wore his military uniform often these days, but when he put it on, he oozed military gorgeous. He was tall, with olive colored skin and chiselled features. Just think powerful, good looking, severely muscular soldier, and that's my Esai.

Even though we had four kids and had been married for quite a few years my heart still skipped a beat when he put on his trunks and strode across our pool deck to the diving board.

I'm not sure which I liked better, watching him execute a graceful dive and slip smoothly into the water or when he easily lifted himself out on the edge of the pool, water cascading over his rippling abs. It was like he was still 24 years old, only much wiser.

He had been on the diving team at his university and did very well on the national stage. He even got a shot at the Olympic team, but he already knew what he wanted for a career and was focused on that.

He was top of his class at Georgetown and knew he wanted to stay that way. He could balance his athletic pursuits, which included football and basketball, with his scholarly requirements but studies always came first.

We met as undergrads there at Georgetown. That was how he ended up in a branch of the military as that was a school at which they frequently scouted for talent. There were always CIA, Army, Air Force and FBI recruiters around the Georgetown campus. Some of the best agents had come from our school.

We discussed the impending birth often. Each of us had ideas and we picked the top qualities of the other and hoped they would be imbued on our little girl.

Esai, saying he wanted her to have my good looks, intelligence and drive to succeed. I would fire back that I hoped she had his body and athletic prowess as well as his toughness and some of his Hispanic sexiness. We both figured that if we somehow had a little girl that was 50/50, having each of our best qualities, she would be a real dynamo.

Turned out she would be all we thought and so much, much more. We found that out very early on too.

Chapter One – Finally, A Girl

We both waited patiently. I had always delivered very close to my due date, and I had no reason to think differently on this one. I was taking the usual ribbing from the other detectives in my squad, and they even had a pool going on the birth date. I, of course, bought a couple of squares right away hoping for the big win. The last pool on me ended with the winner picking up almost three thousand dollars. We were good financially but three grand buys a lot of diapers!

The day finally came, and everything went smoothly. With very little fanfare and not a lot of grunting and moaning our daughter was born. Esai never let go of my hand once. At one point I think I was close to breaking one of his fingers I was squeezing so tightly but I knew he would never let go. He had an extremely high tolerance for pain, almost otherworldly. I thought that if any man could ever stand the pain of childbirth, it would be my Esai.

He held her first and then laid her on my chest where I met the gaze of the most beautiful little baby I had ever seen. She had his dark hair and even on day one seemed to already have her father's facial features.

Interestingly she cried only briefly and then settled down, just laying there like it was just another day.

She had an odd calmness about her, something that would really help her later in life. Don't get me wrong, our sons were each pretty perfect too, but this was different. Even at one day old Megan had already carved out a unique identity for herself within our little family.

Esai was all smiles and the three of us stayed in my room together that night. He left for only a few moments to go out and tell the boys that everything was good. Their new little sister scored a ten on the APGAR scale used to rate the health of new babies.

It is a score used to assess newborns against infant mortality and general health. A typical score was 7, 8 or 9. I looked at Esai and told him and he just smiled at me and said, "that's my girl, less than a day old and already hitting it out of the park."

He was kidding of course, but we would eventually find how prophetic that statement really was.

Chapter Two – Megan, The Early Years

Very early on Megan demonstrated that she was going to be her own person. Even at two years of age she was unafraid of things that usually make toddlers anxious. She would see a large dog, much larger than she, and she would walk up, look at the pooch eye to eye, and give it a huge hug. The dogs never moved. She was like a mini horse-whisperer or something. They must have been able to sense her calmness.

It seemed each day she was doing something and soon saying something that gave you pause for thought. It wasn't so much older than her years or anything like that. It was something different.

As we came to expect, she began to excel at all things physical too. It seemed to make no difference what it was she was always in the top percentiles. Of course, her big brothers all just idolized her. They were her biggest fans right out of the gate. The boys were all very successful athletes in many sports, and they all were strong academically. When it came to "their little sister" it was a whole different ballgame though.

It seemed to make no difference what she did it was a big thing to them. I really believe that is what set her on the path to becoming the powerhouse she became.

She had the best athletic and intellectual upbringing that anyone could experience in my opinion.

It was also ingrained in her from a very young age that when it came to intelligence, sports, and strength there was no such thing as gender. It's a wonder she never became a true tom-boy.

I would like to see her up against some of these "transitioning" males today who suddenly decide to compete against females in university. I have no issues with that community, but it seems like some of these folks are trying to game the system. After all, you developed as a male for nineteen or twenty years.

Their lungs, heart capacity, muscles etc, have all been male for most of their life. I don't think one year of testosterone blockers will have much effect. I just read about a university swimmer who was male, transitioned and is now competing against females and breaking all kinds of NCAA Women's records. I'd like to see him face off against my Megan today! He would be in for a shock.

Back to today. Megan still did little girl things when growing up though. I recall her first dance recital.

She was only four and entered a competition. She did not win a medal and came off the stage in tears. I watched as she ran up to Esai crying. He whispered something to her. She stepped back, smiled, and threw down the participation ribbon and firmly stated, "next time I will do so well they will HAVE to give me a medal." That was our little Megan.

That was the last time we saw tears at anything resembling a competition. She did very well in school, both academically and athletically.

I would look at her commitment, bravery and talent and wish that I could have been more like her as a child. Fact was I was a bit of a late bloomer academically, only hitting my stride later in high school.

Although Esai was busy doing all things military and I was often swamped as a Boston PD Detective there was always one of us at her many events. It was in the eighth grade when she really started to distance herself from the pack. Prior to that there were other kids that were her equal or could even best her at certain things.

When the eighth grade hit, she was suddenly on another planet. The boys had spent a lot of time with her after the seventh grade and it really got her to the next level. A solid honors student, she still found time to compete in many sports.

Her father and I had a few discussions with the school, end even had to make a few threats, to ensure she could always face the best competition. Once, we had to lobby and threaten the school board to get her on the boys' basketball team and the boys soccer team too. She clearly had no equals and no competition in the girl's sports. I was supportive of women's athletics to be sure, but in Megan's case I was worried the lack of competition might kill her drive.

Of course, she excelled at those sports and more. The one she really took to quickly though were the martial arts. I suppose with her brothers teaching her tricks from Jiu Jitsu, Judo and Taekwondo to protect her from boys, that should have been expected.

They were always working with Megan, who by now had evolved into quite a young talent. Also, as she was taller than all but the tallest boys, she could already kick box with the best. Even at the age of fourteen her kicks were works of art, smooth powerful and deadly accurate.

However, Judo quickly became her favorite. In no time, she was an accomplished Judoka. She immediately understood the concept of leverage and was executing almost-perfect throws right out of the gate. Again, the boys had a big impact on that. They showed her how to submit almost anyone of almost any size in numerous ways.

So, here we had an eighth-grade girl, competing against boys in almost everything, who quickly became very skilled in multiple martial arts. We were very surprised when she was sent home from a party for hurting some boy though. Megan had always been taught never to be the aggressor and in all cases to try and talk people out of trouble. We understood the damage she could do and the trouble it could get her into.

It was your typical eighth grade mixed party, nerdy boys and awkward girls. It was all girls and boys she knew, and the parents knew each other too. It was just your run-of-the-mill junior high get together. That was up until I received a call that she had hurt one of the other kids and I would have to come get her.

Esai was away on a mission, and I was not too thrilled about my evening getting cut short. I knocked gently on the door when I arrived, and Megan was sitting in the kitchen.

She was wise enough to not start yakking right away, she saved it for the car. I let the mom tell me what she was told, I apologized, and we left. I had an inkling what really happened so was not at all surprised when I asked Meg what went on. She had never lied to me, and I knew she wasn't about to start.

She told me one of the boys had come up to her and grabbed her, so she stopped him.

I had to supress my grin when she told me he grabbed her chest, so she grabbed his head in a Brazilian Jiu Jitsu move. Typically. one would then bring a knee into the attackers' chin and that would be that. I was REALLY hoping that wasn't what she did.

She went on to tell me that seeing as how he seemed to want some attention for his little penis, he got it. She drove her knee into his groin, and he collapsed crying. The other kids lied saying Megan started it and that was it, she was on her way home. I was disappointed that none of the other girls stood up for her and backed her version of events.

That was a valuable lesson for us both. Megan needed to better appreciate her strength and agility. With the confidence that you COULD defeat someone, frequently a physical confrontation could be avoided.

We discussed it at length on our drive and again when her father returned home. She needed to call on that sense of calm that she was born with before resorting to using her strength.

Chapter Three – High School

I really enjoyed myself in junior high, but I was ready for high school. There would be kids from three other junior highs coming together with our school. I was excited to have a whole new group of friends and basically a fresh start.

As always, I poured myself into everything school related. I continued my honor student ways while joining all the teams I wanted to join. My parents always told me that provided my grades remained high I could try any sport. In my first year, I was forced to play basketball on the girl's team, which did not thrill me. Sure, it was great to meet new teammates and make friends, but the competition was not what I was used to.

By the time our season started I was already the best player on the team and the go-to girl when we had to have points. As a freshman that was certainly not typical. Based on the formulas the school board used they tried to force me to play Junior Varsity but that didn't last too long. I got a special dispensation from the school board after the Director of Athletics saw me play and was quietly promoted to Varsity.

Unfortunately, I still got bored very quickly. There was really no competition for me, so I immediately started lobbying to play on the boy's team.

Title IX was old news by now and women's sports, in both high school and university, were on more equal footing but that didn't affect the level of competition during my time there. It did nothing to help my cause.

I was permitted to continue to play on the varsity team, but we started to make it known that if I was not allowed to play on the boy's teams, I would cease to play all high school sports. A little extra pressure might help sway their minds. My parents said it was a good lesson for me to understand the leverage I had and how to best use it.

I had also joined the girl's lacrosse team and the tennis team and dominated those too. I don't want to sound too cocky, but I was helping to put our school on the map. Alumni donations were rolling in and by the time I started the eleventh grade I regularly saw scouts from multiple sports at my games. They were barred from talking to students but that did not stop them from watching a game or a match.

My high school sports career was extremely busy and often I would go from a game in one sport directly to a practice for another! Between Basketball, soccer, and lacrosse, I was a whirlwind of athletics. I have since wondered how I did it and still maintained a 4.0 GPA. I suppose I really did thrive under pressure although I never felt what normal people would call pressure. It was always just one more challenge for me.

I knew I would have my pick of schools if I wanted but I also knew I would be attending Georgetown. Nothing to do with their notable grads that included Bill Clinton, Judge Scalia, and Bradley Cooper but because they had a very strong Foreign Service school and great athletics.

Of course, it didn't hurt that I was a legacy there either.

The cost was prohibitive, even if you could qualify for aid. I could not. At almost $51,000 per year, Georgetown is one of the priciest universities in the states. Nevertheless, I knew I would go there, one way or the other.

My parents wanted me to fully appreciate the cost of an education and I always knew that I would be paying for one half of it. I would need to apply for my own loans unless I was able to secure scholarships.

That was my goal. I applied for, and worked toward, every scholarship and bursary that I could find. If it wasn't based on financial need, I was applying! Anything that I qualified for academically I went after, and all my practice and training was designed to get me access to sports scholarships as well.

It helped tremendously when, after my father did some lobbying, I was permitted to play basketball and soccer for the boy's teams in high school. It would do nothing to get me onto the men's teams when I did get to Georgetown, but I was a shoo-in and full ride scholarship candidate for the ladies' teams. That was when I was still in the eleventh grade! There could be nothing official but with my parents' connections and friends they had I knew I had no worries.

I just had to continue on the academic track I was on and add in more AP and IB courses whenever I could. The International Baccalaureate (IB) program in high school was designed to challenge the best of the best and better prepare you for a university education. The courses were challenging but you had a great deal of leeway to create while you learned. I excelled in that type of environment.

I was certain that I would want to attend either the Walsh School of Foreign Service or the McCourt School of Public Policy when I got to Georgetown.

I would have the opportunity to study our government, learn multiple foreign languages and soak up everything that attending Georgetown meant.

Georgetown also happens to be the oldest (established in 1789) Catholic and Jesuit university in the nation. It is also where my father and mother received their educations. Both were highly regarded alumni of Georgetown.

I suppose it made sense in a university based on faith and public service as they each had distinguished themselves in their respective areas. I knew my parents would be thrilled when I committed to their Alma Mater. I hoped the NCAA did not create some issue with my decision.

Chapter Four – Georgetown

The time came to sign a letter of intent. In the most anti-climactic signing ever, I expressed my desire to commit to Georgetown. I did have other scholarship offers but with Georgetown I would be where I wanted to be and incur very little debt. I was awarded a full ride scholarship for basketball and soccer. I would also beg my way onto the lacrosse team but that took more effort than I thought. The coach was worried that lacrosse was just an "extra" time filler for me. Like I needed anything like that.

I had always loved the combination of skill and contact in lacrosse and only wished they would have played box lacrosse rather than the tamer field version. Box lacrosse was mostly played in Canada and was a whole lot of fun. Imagine taking field lacrosse into a hockey rink, shortening the sticks, and pretty much allowing you to beat the crap out of everyone with that stick. You could even run the goalies if they were wild enough to leave their crease.

Even though those goalies had tons of huge equipment on I knocked a few into next year when I got to play box lacrosse. I had to tone it down quite a bit playing field lacrosse, but I still really enjoyed it.

Academically I was remaining close to the top, somewhat uncharacteristic for a scholarship jock. I loved the studying and learning and needed very little sleep to stay at the top of my game. I really enjoyed soccer and lacrosse, but basketball was my passion.

As a sophomore and playing on NCAA Division 1 teams, I was having the best university experience ever.

In the Big East we played against other renowned universities including Villanova, Seton Hall, St John's, and DePaul. Instead of the Big East it should been called the ACC - All Catholic Conference! I found that interesting. I wasn't heading off to church every Sunday or anything, but I did appreciate the concept.

Anyway, I did very well on all those teams and loved my athletic career at Georgetown. It was a tremendous experience. I was very proud when I was named an Academic All-American.

The academic side was every bit as exciting for me as sports. Studying foreign policy, I was able to learn so much about the political and socio-economic aspects of many other countries and regions, as well as my own USA.

There was also the language side of things. I was fluent in English and Spanish thanks to my parents. I audited a couple of 200 and 300 Spanish classes and quickly decided to challenge the courses. I was able to think in both languages rather than think in one and convert to another, so it was easy for me to pass those courses.

That allowed me to focus on some others including French, Russian and German. Languages came to me quite easily and by the time I was ready to gather up my degree and head into the world I was fluent in seven of them!

I had never stopped participating in the martial arts either. I retained my Judoka status and grew in that sport. I had gone full force into kick boxing and Brazilian Jiu Jitsu too.

I would have killed it in the MMA if I had wanted to but just before graduation my life took a somewhat unexpected turn.

Chapter Five – Drafted, Sort Of...

I was in my final quarter of school. I had accumulated tons of awards and championships in multiple sports, but my heart was in academics and the martial arts. I suppose I saw both of those as something I could do forever. It was those two areas that made me feel happiest about my life so far.

I was training in the gym, lifting fairly heavy, when I was approached by a woman who said she was with the Navy. She introduced herself, mentioned she knew of my father and asked if we could have coffee. I agreed and told her I just had to finish my workout. She smiled and said she knew I would say that. We agreed to meet at a Starbuck's just off campus.

I rolled in there about an hour later and spotted her sitting in the corner. She stood and shook my hand and said that before we could talk about anything, I would need to sign a confidentiality agreement. I was taken aback by her request but found myself reading the document word for word before I signed anyway.

This was a SERIOUS piece of paper. I cannot reveal the contents, but it was easy to tell she wanted to discuss something very big.

She asked if I had any questions, I said I did not. I signed the document and slid it over in front of her.

She began by telling me an awful lot about myself including my sports career, academic studies and even my MMA pursuits.

This lady knew a LOT about me, and it was a little scary to be honest. I was never a fan of the whole big brother thing.

She went on to explain that she was in a branch of the Navy, and they thought I would be a perfect fit. She told me I would be able to serve my country but still lead a relatively normal life. Other than basic training, I would likely never be in a uniform.

She provided some vague details on operations in other parts of the world as well as within North America. As she was speaking, I was finding it odd that she seemed to be discussing things that could be Navy but also CIA and FBI areas of interest.

The CIA and FBI are both members of the United States Intelligence Community. The CIA has no law enforcement angle and works on gathering information on foreign countries and their citizens. The CIA is barred from collecting information on U.S. citizens including resident aliens and legal immigrants.

On the other hand, the FBI focusses on all things internal to the U.S. and is wholly law enforcement. On paper, the two should never run into each other.

That was not exactly what this lady was laying out. She went on to make clear that should I decide to accept I would first go to a standard US Navy boot camp. I would be unable to tell anyone about this conversation or how I ended up there. I would have to go enlist at a recruiting office like anyone else to eliminate any chance of anyone finding out. We discussed many more things over the course of almost two hours. I asked when I had to give her my answer and she smiled and said tomorrow morning will be fine.

I suppose they wanted to ensure that people were 100% committed so that made sense to me.

She stood, shook my hand, and said she would meet me here at 9:00 AM.

Chapter Six – The Decision

I left the coffee shop, my head reeling from all the information she had shared. I recalled her look, powerful like me. I thought she could certainly hold her own in the octagon. She was clearly also well educated, although she was a Villanova grad, so we were sort of sworn enemies on the field. Not sure I could overlook that!

I slept soundly considering the weight of my decision. I was permitted to tell no one about our discussion, the offer or what I might be doing. My father was a senior guy in the military and was involved in serious business so I was surprised I couldn't even tell him. I could only share information in the vaguest of terms and would be best to simply stick to "I'm joining the Navy."

I awoke and knew that what she had said was what I wanted to do. It would be only 8 to 10 years and would provide me with a comfortable pension for life, including all medical coverage too. I did the math and realized that at the age of 33 or 34 I would be finished, have a nice nest egg already built up and a pretty good fully indexed, pension. The pension would have nothing to do with my income nor would it be taxed in any way. It would be like free money, although I really had no idea how much I would have to sacrifice over the next 8 or 10 years to get that.

It really was an offer too good to be true. I was still skeptical as I stepped through the door of the Starbuck's the next morning at 8:55 AM. She stood and we shook hands. She asked if I was in and when I said yes, she reminded me of the NDA I had signed. Then she slid a relatively simple agreement across the table to me.

Two measly pages and it appeared the government would own me for the near future. They would be pay me well and there was the pension but nevertheless, I would be 100% theirs. I read it closely and noted they already had my complete banking information detailing the amount of the direct deposits that would commence the day I started boot camp. It was sort of like those personal services contracts you used to hear about in the sports world, before the athletes took back control of their own destiny.

I had to initial a couple of spots, as did she, and then a man in a dark suit joined us. He sat down, witnessed our signatures, confirmed the payments and payment information and that was that. She took their copy, and I took mine. I went straight to the bank and put it into my safety deposit box. Before arriving, I stopped to scan it and email to a private email account I had set up at local computer café. No sense taking chances.

She indicated I had one month to enroll. I should get my affairs in order, tell my parents I was joining the Navy, and get prepared for the adventure of a lifetime.

As I walked back home, I was suddenly hit with the reality and weight of the decision I had just made. I wondered what my parents would think when I told them what I was doing.

I thought my father will be impressed on the service side but not sure what mom would think. I sat at the table that evening with my parents and told them I had decided I wanted to join the Navy. Our whole family had served in one way or another, so I wanted to as well. They were quite shocked to say the least. They clearly knew I was a top-flight athlete and could have competed in the Olympics. They also knew that I could approach many companies, even our government, and be hired immediately.

I explained, as best I could, the reasons for my decision and they began to come around a little bit. My mother highlighted the tense state of world affairs and the fact our current President did not seem particularly war averse. Of course, when you think about it, none of them truly were anyway.

The hawks were everywhere in the government, both republicans and democrats. I knew there was nothing I could do, other than follow my orders when I got them. It would soon be my sworn duty.

Chapter Seven – Boot Camp

I went to a recruiting office and enlisted in the Navy. I was told there was only one location the Navy trains its recruits and that was the Great Lakes Naval Training Center, on the shores of Lake Michigan. It is relatively close to Chicago, so not as isolated as a couple of the army boot camps. The naval recruit training command processes more than 50,000 recruits through navy boot camp EVERY year! At least that is how many start!

After all the paperwork was done, I was given a date and time to report at the centre from where I would be transported to GLNTC. I asked for one month to prepare and get my things in order and that was acceptable to them. The recruiters forewarn you that you need to be in top shape physically and mentally to make it through. If you do smoke, you are told to quit now.

I went through the Armed Services Vocational Aptitude test (ASVAB) which is how the Navy determines where they believe you will best fit. Along with all the physical challenges and attempts to cull the herd you learn and practice many skills.

The first few days at the Recruit Training Center (RTC, they love their acronyms) is packed with activity.

The first thing you are issued is Navy sweatsuits. At that point you pack up all your civilian clothing and any non-listed personal items and send them home or donate them to charity.

Immediately after that you pee in a cup and a comprehensive drug screen is completed. If anything shows up you are done, no matter which state you're from that happened to legalize marijuana.

Your typical schedule begins the next day at 6:00 AM and goes to 10:00 PM. I was surprised to find out that while things like uniforms, hygiene items , shoe polish and some other things are given to you, you had to pay for many other items. I guess they don't give you EVERYTHING you need.

All recruits then get assigned to a division of about 80 men and women. These divisions live in 1,000 person dormitories called "ships". While men and women train side by side they do not room together. There are female sections and male sections. They co-exist but are encouraged not to mingle.

The first task completed is the designation of recruit leaders, know as Recruit Petty Officers.

The RPO's ensure that there is good order, discipline, and security within their division. I was designated an RPO because I was what they called "squared away". I seemed on my way.

During the rest of this first week, known as "P" week, you learned many seemingly mundane tasks. Tasks key to defeating an enemy, I'm sure. Things such as the correct way to make a bed, fold underwear, iron uniforms. Oh well, you HAD to start somewhere as far as discipline goes.

Many recruits arrive with NO discipline, hoping the forces will somehow "give" it to them. The Navy has more classroom time than the other branches of the military. You learn the Uniform Code of Military Justice, standards of conduct, discrimination, and of course the 11 General Orders.

Stirring stuff.

The first full week of boot camp focuses on establishing physical conditioning levels along with some pretty intense classroom topics. While you are qualifying in swimming, drownproofing and other things aquatic you also spend time in class. Topics covered in this first week included rank recognition, rape awareness, sexual harassment, fraternization, and core values of the Navy.

With all that, the physical training is by far the focus. You are up at 6:00 AM and many times plunged into a cold pool to swim laps, practice rescue techniques and learn how to save others. That may be followed immediately by serious cardio exercises and then right back into a cold pool to test your stamina and ability to recover. This was clearly not for the faint of heart. I watched as recruits dropped out, even after only one week.

There are things like the boot camp confidence course where you work in teams of four. It simulates obstacles one might encounter in a shipboard emergency such as fire. You are carrying heavy life support and rescue equipment and scrambling through small openings. I knew the biggest thing here was to finish as a team, so I was focussed on that. The Navy did not want anyone who could or would operate in a "save themselves" mode.

It wasn't until the fourth week where I saw an opportunity to fully display my strength and power. The physical fitness test is standard for all recruits. Much like American Ninja Warrior, the course was the same for males and females. I was more than ready to find out where I stacked up against the hundreds currently training.

The physical fitness test was as basic as it gets. Sit-reaches, curl-ups, push-ups and a 1.5-mile run.

There were some ripped dudes and gals to be sure, but I was able to rise to the top, thanks mostly to a blazing mile and a half run. I held my own in the other areas, but the run is what got me to the top.

Basic training is basic training and that is exactly what it was. I started to wonder why I had signed up. During week eight there is still physical training and classroom, but you finally got to put on your dress uniform and make that final pass-in-review. I was a little surprised at the feelings that washed over me when I looked at myself in my dress uniform for the first time.

I thought of my father, my uncles and aunts, my grandfather, all of whom served in the military in one branch or another. My chest swelled with pride. I wondered what was next.

Everyone, including me, was certain I would be off to "A School",
what the Navy calls its technical school. I watched as other, less skilled
people than myself, walked over to that building. That was the first
time I opened my "orders" and noted that I was directed to a different
location.

When I arrived, I was told that I was to be the first female to ever
receive the training I was about to receive.

Navy SEALs are known as the finest trained Special Forces soldiers
in the military. Almost everything you have likely read about them is
true.

What you also may have noticed is this is exclusively a male pursuit.
There are no female operators. That was why my transport had an
interesting second passenger. Although he was dressed in civilian
clothes, I recognized Vice Admiral Robert Bourque as the other
occupant. He introduced himself when I got into the vehicle, and I did
my best to salute.

He said I was a very important person now and that soon I would go
through additional screening known as the SEAL Officer Assessment
and Selection program. If I was able to pass that I would be accepted
into Basic Underwater Demolition/SEAL training, known as BUD/
S training. He asked what I knew, and I had to admit very little other
than what I had seen online.

He went on to explain that I would remain at Great Lakes and complete this screening. It included diver training, explosive ordnance, and special warfare boat operator courses. ALL candidates, men or women go through the same training. He also noted that I would receive NO breaks or special attention. If anything, it might be tougher on me than the males.

He pointed out there were no guarantees. I did not get to this point because I was a woman. I got this far despite being a woman. He said it would be difficult but an amazing accomplishment if I made it through.

Almost 1,000 recruits each year entered the assessment phase and only 10% of those move on to BUD/S training. Of that group only 10% complete the challenge and become SEALs. TEN, ten out of a thousand!

I found his remarks off-putting but also immediately motivating. He may have thought he knew who he was dealing with, but he had no idea of how capable I am.

Chapter Eight – Basic Underwater Demolition Training

I blew through the assessment to even be allowed to TRY and complete the BUD/S program. NSW PREP is the acronym for Naval Special Warfare Preparatory School. It is designed to improve your readiness to move to the next level and weed out the weakest who, by the way, are still tougher than 96% of the population!

It was not easy but not nearly as difficult as I had expected. The assessment played into many of my strengths especially swimming, hand to hand combat and marksmanship. I excelled in hand-to-hand combat thanks to my brothers and all the other training I had. I submitted or disarmed male after male and I was getting attention from superiors already.

I suppose some of that early attention may have been because I was a bit of a novelty to them. If those thoughts existed, they were only in their minds and not mine. I KNEW what I could do and had all the determination I required to prove it to them.

I successfully completed the program, and I was slated to start BUD/S training after four days of liberty. This portion was conducted in California. I was pumped.

I was still operating in a vacuum but the lady who I initially signed with warned me of that. I would be on my own until they deemed the time was right. I was simply to excel and achieve.

I enjoyed my four days, did a little surfing and swimming, and then reported to camp. The SEAL trainers are famous for claiming that their training is 90% mental. Certainly, the ability to hang in there is critical but still, claiming the BUD/S school is 90% mental is a bit of a stretch. At least I thought it was a stretch at this point in time.

The BUD/S training is 24 weeks and then you have another 28-week SEAL qualification training program you must pass as well. I immediately set my goal to be in that 1% that completes it all.

BUD/S training kicks off with another appropriately named "hell week". Five days of constant physical training and challenges. You get only four hours sleep per night and were constantly encouraged to quit, take the easy way out, give up, known as "ringing the bell."

I think those training leaders might be judged on how many of these DOR's (Drop On Request) they can get. That cynicism may have come from my view of the basic forces overall.

I would soon learn that they were simply doing their utmost to guarantee that only the best survived.

There was no way I was going to DOR. Giving up has never been in my nature. I watched others, in that first week, drop out though. Many people have a breaking point they have never met. If you have never pushed through when you thought you must give up, then you never discovered what you can truly accomplish. You never understood the momentary pain required to achieve the massive gain if you persisted in continuing.

Whether it was doing curl-ups in teams while holding a massive log or standing in cold water to the waist waiting for orders, I got myself into another zone. I remembered the 90% mental comment and began to understand it and live it each day.

When you are physically at your breaking point it is only your mind that can keep you in the game. Carrying a boat on your head with your team racing through breaking surf, standing in ice cold water for hours, doing curl-ups on the beach as the surf crashed over your head, it was all designed to get those who could not persevere to ring that bell. It didn't matter whether your limitations were physical or mental, if you couldn't "take it" you were done.

The drill sergeants were all cut with the same thread. It still seemed to me like they WANTED you to drop out, they needed you to drop out.

They were skilled at finding anything that could be used against you, any perceived weakness with which to pressure you. They understood they had to produce the best of the best. That was the only way to help guarantee successful missions.

In my case, they thought my weakness was obvious. It was difficult not to laugh when they tried the tired old "daddy's little girl" and "you belong in a dress, not battle fatigues" crap. I just kept a straight face, barked out a "sir, yes sir" each time I was addressed and that was that. I knew that I would power through whatever challenge was presented to me, mental or physical. Standing up to anyone at this point, especially a drill sergeant, could be the end of my journey.

I was going to earn that Special Warfare Insignia, the SEAL Trident, there were simply no other options for me.

I knew that SEAL training was not only about water, even though a common slang term SEALs call themselves is frogmen. The name comes from Sea, Air And Land. It means that Navy SEALs will be expert in all types and manner of military techniques and equipment, and then some. Even the first physical test you must pass before being qualified to enter the BUD/S training is difficult.

You start with significant medical screening to ensure they are getting the best of the best. I think it might also be to avoid people dying during training, that never looks good to the public. At any rate, simply making the minimums on the physical "entry exam" will likely not get you in. As with everything SEAL-related, you must excel.

You must complete the following: a 500-yard swim in nine minutes or less, 90 or more push ups in two minutes or less, 90 or more sit ups in two minutes or less, eighteen pull ups and then a 1.5 mile run in combat boots which must be quicker than 9 and a half minutes. There is minimal rest and recovery time between these challenges, and many don't make it past this.

IF you pass this first series of tests, you then get into the meat of the training and real thinning of the herd. Prep school ends with more physical tests that include a 1,000-yard swim in less than 15 minutes (with fins thankfully), 70 push ups, 10 pull ups and 60 curl ups all in less than two minutes each.

You end that with a four-mile run in boots and pants that must be completed in less than 31 minutes. No idea where they get thirty-ONE minutes, but many more do not make it past this milestone either.

Less than 15% of candidates even make it to the BUD/S segment. There are many brutal and painful physical challenges that are designed to tax your mind and will, while trying to break down your body. Ocean training is a huge component but there are all types of other physical tests involved.

At the same time, you are being pushed to the limit in the classroom learning about tactics, strategy, and all things war. Unless you make it through and achieve high ratings in this phase you are not permitted to enter Seal Qualification Training, known of course as SQT.

While water training is not everything it IS a large component. Imagine your hands and feet bound tightly and then being tossed into a pool to swim underwater to ensure you are drown-proofed. What about still bound and floating for five consecutive minutes? Seals MUST know they can survive virtually any situation in the water. All seals must be able to hold their breath underwater for at least two full minutes.

Even things like knots become brutal tests of stamina and commitment. I wasn't really a knot person, but I knew it was coming so had trained for it. I had already spent hours and hours practicing each one.

You had to tie five different, complicated knots one after another in two minutes or less.

It had to be two minutes or less because you are tying these knots while holding your breath underwater! You are permitted to surface between knots for one single breath, but it is better if you do not surface between every knot. If you can do two on one breath, the trainers notice. Everything you do better than required can give you a slight edge.

After all of this you arrive at the aforementioned Hell Week. To put it into perspective for the average athlete, in a five-day session you run a total of 200 miles while you complete many other brutal physical challenges. Tests are tests and there are similarities between the various levels. It is when you get to phase two that things become a little more "real" however.

Phase Two is referred to as Combat Diving, for very good reason. You are to swim various distances under differing circumstances, but at all times, you must be prepared for an attack. While completing a two-mile open ocean swim you will be attacked by one of your instructors and must "win" that challenge. You are also taught how to rescue non cooperative possible drowning victims.

Another test involves swimming submerged with full SCUBA gear. An instructor sneaks up behind you, yanks the regulator out of your mouth and ties your oxygen lines in a knot.

Every part of you starts thinking you are about to die, but you must remain calm and cool. You must follow the procedure to get your gear back in working order.

This happens over and over, for at least 20 minutes. At least you get four attempts and 80% of people need them.

Only one in five people successfully complete the "pool comp" on the first try.

Once you do beat all these challenges you move on to Phase Three (Land Warfare) where you are sent to a remote island for seven weeks and train with live ammunition and explosives. More training and studying and becoming proficient in weapons and demolition and then off you go for these live drills.

Again, long days with virtually no sleep taxes every bit of who you are. The whole saga tests every part of your being. The punishments for even the slightest of errors are severe. Most claim this is the most dangerous phase of training, both for yourself and those around you.

It is not as dangerous as the required parachute training though. That is where there have been more than one or two accidental deaths.

You free fall in increasing distances until at the end you are jumping out of an aircraft from 9,500 feet up and deploying your chute at the last possible moment.

Oh, did I mention this all happens AT NIGHT?

IF you can complete all of this you are finally awarded the chance to enter SQT, Seal Qualification Training. I completed this phase too, not as easily as the initial testing but that is how it was supposed to work. You may excel in one area but that was never enough, you had to be at the top in everything!

Chapter 9 – SQT

Here I was, still standing and about to begin Seal Qualification Training. I had met my own expectations and I am certain exceeded the trainers' expectations of me.

Now it was time to acquire the tactical knowledge needed to operate as a SEAL. SQT is an intense 26 weeks, and I knew this might be my most difficult. The others saw what I could do, and they now knew I had the tenacity to survive and the will to win. That wasn't going to be the issue.

I believed I would have multiple hurdles to overcome. Some would think I was "weaker" than a man and they needed to protect me, therefore jeopardizing their own safety. That would likely get us both tossed. Some would push me harder than ever and think they could break me. Again, the results would not be good. There would be one, two, maybe three or four who would respect my skills and ability. They would know I am their equal and would treat me as such.

I needed to quickly identify those teammates and very subtly align myself with them. Ensure we were close to one another during drills and testing.

I needed to show the leaders that I could both be on a team and someday lead a team. I also had to prove that I would be accepted in whichever role I was cast within a team.

I had to do all this while continuing to learn and try to be top of class in as many areas as I could. SQT included more weapons training and small unit tactics. There was also demolition, cold weather, medical and maritime operations components one had to learn forward and backward.

One of the most important sections was SERE training. SERE training was the acronym for Survival, Evasion, Resistance and Escape. These were all absolute requirements to become a SEAL.

As a female I may have some unique challenges, but I was determined to avoid capture most of all. The other area I spent significant extra time on was escape. I knew that I could be subjected to torture of who knows what type, so I had to prepare myself mentally and physically to defeat captors and get away.

I also had great focus when it came to weapons training. There were all kinds of traditional weapons and many more common items that could be weaponized, if you knew what you were doing. This is where I acquired my taste for the garotte. You can make one from all kinds of common items.

Basically, you needed two handles and a length of rope or wire. It was a quiet weapon and could be used many ways and from many positions. It was also very easy to hide.

Things were going smoothly for me. I had found the people I needed to work with, and our leader formed us into a small tactics group. I learned form them and I like to think they learned from me as well.

They really DO yell out HUA, pronounced Hoo-Ah, meaning Heard, Understood and Acknowledged. I saw it more than once on military related shows and movies but was a little surprised they actually DID say it.

One of their favorite sayings is "the only easy day was yesterday." This one has deep meaning for every SEAL. It is as much about preparedness as it is understanding the challenges ahead may be your most difficult yet.

"Don't run to your death" is another saying that reminds you that restraint is often the best policy. In the old days of war many men simply ran bravely ahead, only to be shot and killed. This is now viewed as stupidity or recklessness, not bravery. This restraint, calmness and planning is driven into you every day during and after SEAL training. This motto, almost more than any other, has kept many SEALs on the right side of the soil.

My personal favorite is "no plan survives first contact with the enemy". Mike Tyson (not my favorite male of course) co-opted this one when he quipped, "Everyone has a plan until they get punched in the mouth." The key to this one is that you must always be agile, and adaptive when leading an operation. You must always plan and consider multiple possibilities because an inability to adapt and change can get you killed. After all, the other side is planning too.

I eased myself to sleep that night with the thought that I was about to receive my Trident pin, the symbol that you were now a Navy SEAL. I had almost made it and I was extremely proud of myself.

We were a week out from the end of this phase, and I had excelled in many areas. I had completely immersed myself in the concepts and operations of a SEAL member within a SEAL team. I had almost forgotten there was an end goal other than me succeeding. I had always assumed, since my meeting with Vice Admiral Bourque, they WANTED a female Navy SEAL.

I would soon find out that was not the case at all. He knew what I was doing there, and I believe he hoped I would fail. The SEALs were no more ready for a woman operator now than they were ten or twenty years ago.

Whether they were ready or not, I knew that I WAS ready! I fully believed that fact would trump all others. I suppose this was an area where the positive support and training from my whole family had a bit of a negative effect. It seemed that in many minds, equality would never be truly achieved.

Chapter Ten – The Disappearance

I went out for an early morning run before roll call and was racing through the grounds. I was on a high knowing that I had made it. I was soon to become a SEAL.

It was a cool, clear morning with dew on the ground and the sun soon began to rise. I had entered a calm phase of my run when everything simply seems effortless. At this point I always felt like I could go forever. My body operated like I was out for a casual walk, expending very little energy.

In my mind, everything simply slowed down. I always had a clarity at this point, about almost anything I considered. If I had major decisions to make it was often done during one of these solo runs.

I rounded a bend past a thicket of trees and there, standing in my path, was the lady who had originally signed me up. I stopped and she simply said, "it is time." I asked what she meant by that, and she said that I had to leave immediately. It was like someone hit me in the chest with a hammer. I couldn't believe that they wanted me to stop short of my goal. She said we needed to go talk elsewhere and she led me to a waiting vehicle.

As we approached the blacked-out Escalade, the rear door opened and there sat Vice Admiral Bourque. I asked what was going on and he looked me in the eye and congratulated me. He said he had watched my progress and was very impressed. He, not too convincingly, said that he wished I could continue as a SEAL, but he was informed the country had a greater need for me elsewhere.

He shook my hand and then pulled the trident from his pocket and pressed it into my other hand. It was anti-climactic receiving my trident this way. It lacked the pomp, circumstance, and camaraderie of when you typically were awarded your trident. It was smaller than I expected but the weight of it was immense, at least in my mind if not in my hand.

This would usually happen at SQT graduation. You had begun your training almost a year ago at this point surviving BUD/s and now SQT. It was the most memorable of times for all SEALs. Your teammates were all with you. You felt the bond. You were finally a team, soon to be forged into a brotherhood on the field of battle.

The Trident pin itself displays the three areas where SEALs operate, Sea, Air and Land. The anchor signifies the Navy and above that is an eagle with outstretched wings symbolizing the air and strength and courage.

The eagle's right talon grips a Trident implying Neptune, the Roman God and ruler of the sea. In the left talon there is a ready-to-fire flintlock pistol. This represents a SEAL's constant state of readiness.

He then handed me a KA-BAR knife. This is awarded at the same ceremony to each graduate. To symbolize the sacrifice that came before them, each knife is engraved with the name of a Navy SEAL who was killed in action. Even those who were killed in training are remembered in this unique way. This knife is sometimes used by SEALs but more often kept only as a memento. It is larger than most fighters prefer, carrying a seven-inch blade and being almost a foot long. That being said, many do acquire the same style knife to use in combat. It can be very effective in close quarters.

The Ka-Bar has a razor-sharp section of curved blade behind which there is a serrated edge. The knife slices easily through flesh in the first four inches with the last three inches serrated to the bolster ripping and tearing to immobilize an attacker when used correctly. I looked closely at the knife and noted the name, Stephen Mills. The date was August 6th, 2011. I recalled seeing his photograph on the wall, a bearded powerful-looking man. His eyes seemed to carry a knowledge that he could do anything, anywhere at any time he wanted.

It was not lost on me that Mills was supposedly the leader of SEAL team 6's gold squadron, also know as DEVGRU. They were killed when Afghan insurgents shot down the Chinook transport helicopter they were in. It was one of the largest losses in SEAL history with 17 SEALS, 15 operators and two bomb specialists dying in the crash. 2 others also died that fateful night.

We had learned about this mission during tactical and strategic training. It was in the Tangi valley, about 80 miles outside of Kabul, where it happened. The same place where Alexander The Great lost so many men. A US Special Ops team had been in a firefight for almost two hours when reinforcements were called in.

A CH-47 transport helicopter, Extortion 17, was carrying the team and others, including Afghan commandoes and a US military dog. As the helo approached the target area it was attacked by insurgents and crashed, killing everyone aboard. This loss was the single largest loss of life of US forces since the war in Afghanistan began way back in 2001.

It was the single most devastating day in SEAL Team 6 history, one every SEAL carried with them.

It is taught in SQT because of the many decisions that came before the tragic moment. Although all operational decisions related to this horror were deemed "tactically sound" there were many issues discussed after the fact.

I think it was just astounding to people involved that such a powerful force could be taken out with one simple RPG (Rocket Propelled Grenade). One man, laying on the ground close to the landing area simply waited for the helo to get close enough. He likely stood or got to his knees, aimed, and pulled the release that sent the destructive projectile on its way.

SEAL team 6 family members blamed the US government. They claimed when the government announced that ST 6 had been the ones who killed Bin Laden, they placed a target on them. Secrecy was what kept SEALs and other special operators somewhat safe. This need to brag and tell citizens who took out Bin Laden may have contributed to the deaths of so many brave Americans. There was even talk this was an inside job with Afghan forces tipping off the Taliban.

We shouldn't assume that was NOT the case, after all the US is not the only country with war skills, including spies. I decided immediately that I would not use this knife. I would put it in a safe place. Maybe, when I was done, I might get the image tattooed on me but that was a decision to be made many years down the road.

General Bourque looked me in the eyes, and I thought I saw pride, or perhaps envy. He congratulated me again and then got out of the vehicle and went to his own car. That was it, I knew I would likely never see him again.

So, there I sat somewhat dumbfounded and more than a little pissed off. She then told me that I was to go to an apartment that was rented in my name. I had a gym membership there and everything I would need to live.

I was permitted to meet my parents, but she would make all the arrangements.

It was all pretty dark stuff to me, and I had some concerns. She said that my "handler" would contact me. He was the only person I would ever take orders from and the only person I should trust, no matter what I heard or read. She warned that in a perfect world, she and my handler would be the only people who would know I existed, besides a few others "like me".

It was good to know there were more of me, others I could perhaps meet and talk to at some point. It wouldn't be like a SEAL team, but I hoped it would indeed be a team.

Chapter Eleven – What's Next?

I finally met my handler who went only by the name of Cato. The only other time I had heard that name was Kato (with a "k") belonging to Kato Kaelin, who was a witness in the O.J.Simpson trial.

He seemed a little younger than I expected, maybe in his forties but could have been a young-looking fifties kind of guy. Afterwards I came to learn his name (not his real one of course) is of Latin origin and means "intelligent and all-knowing". In Roman history Cato the Elder (originally born as Marcus Porcius Cato) was a deep-thinking Roman diplomat during Caesar's rule. He was a soldier but was known as Cato the Elder, Cato the Wise, and Cato the Ancient.

We agreed that if I was ever in trouble from which I could not extricate myself and I was able to somehow contact him that I would use the name Marcus instead of Cato. He added, knowing the history of the name, that this name was assigned to him and not one he picked. He thought that would be just a little narcissistic I supposed.

He confirmed that I was aware that everything I did was to be done in complete secrecy. He said again that he would be my only contact and the only person from whom I would receive orders, direction, or guidance.

He said he would arrange for me to meet with my parents, and I was only to tell them I was on a Special Forces team. Absolutely no other details could be shared with them, or anyone else.

I asked if he needed their contact information and he laughed, quickly rattling off my parents' full names, where each was employed and what they typically did on weekends. I was a little surprised but not shocked as I had a rough idea what I was getting into.

He said he would arrange the meeting in three days and would bring my parents and me to a neutral location. I would be permitted no contact after that point until I was advised by him that I could. He explained that when I was finished, I would be taken directly to an aircraft. That aircraft would take me to the next phase of my training.

I slept fitfully that evening, knowing that week I would see and speak to my parents for the last time in a long time. Cato called me as I returned from the gym and said I would be having lunch with my parents the next day. He said all the arrangements were made and a car would pick me up at 11:30 AM. I had my story straight, but I knew my parents would surely know that I was not being completely honest. Being who they were, they would also know not to ask about details.

I emerged from my door at precisely 11:30 and there was a sedan sitting out front. The passenger window rolled down and the driver simply said, "Cato sent me to get you." I got into the back seat and rode in silence until the car stopped out front of a small restaurant in Chinatown. I couldn't help but see this as an odd location. I thanked the driver and got out.

As I stepped through the door Cato greeted me and ushered me to a private room in the rear of the restaurant where my parents were waiting.

We hugged, sat back down and the questions started coming at me like wind-driven rain. Calm down, calm down I told them, and they both relaxed just a bit.

Before they could start in on me, I told them there were only certain topics I could discuss. The only thing I could tell them about my work was that I was in a Special Forces division. I told them we would have limited contact for I didn't know how long but I would be thinking about them all the time.

We ate and talked for at least two hours, sharing many stories about my brothers. I could tell they were both concerned. I let them know that if anything happened to me, they would be kept informed and while they would not know where I was or what I was doing they would know I was safe. I also needed them to understand that I would be doing what was best for my country. Just like they had done.

That was it. We hugged and they left out the front door while Cato came and got me, and we left out the back. We got into a blacked-out SUV and began driving. I assumed we would be going to the main airport but that wasn't the case. When the car stopped, we were at what appeared to be a rural airstrip. There was a small sized executive aircraft sitting there. It said it was a Beechcraft, Super King Air. Twin turbo props so I knew it had decent range and was almost as fast as a small jet.

He shook my hand at the door of the aircraft and said there was a parachute on my seat. I was off to receive more training and this training would also be my final evaluation. If I passed, I was in and I was his. If I failed, this would be the last time we would see one another. I was to put the parachute on and wait until the pilot told me to jump. As the door closed and I took my seat the pilot said we had at least an hour to the drop zone so he would let me know when to put the parachute on. That was much better, sitting in a seat while wearing one of those for any length of time can be a real pain.

We flew in silence and, as all the windows were blacked out, I had no idea which direction we were headed. I couldn't be sure, but it felt like we were in the air for five hours or more.

The pilot had said there was a small fridge with water and snacks and that I might want to have something during our flight. I had a bottle of water in front of me and was snacking on a sandwich when he finally said we were about 45 minutes from the drop zone.

I looked closely at the parachute, familiar with the model. They were directional chutes that you could control and fly in almost any situation. I checked it over as I had some trepidation that I had not packed my own chute. It was a tedious task but one that every jumper preferred to do his or herself. It gave you confidence knowing your equipment was prepared with detail and your life was in your own hands.

The pilot yelled back that we were now five minutes from the drop area. I would have to quickly spot a flare as I jumped and head for that location. With the chute hanging from the front of me and my full pack, including weapons on my back, I was carrying close to 90 pounds. I readied myself and moved close to the hatch.

A red light flashed, and the door began to open in front of me. I held tightly onto the two rails on either side and prepared myself. Helmet and goggles firmly secured, chute at the ready I watched the light. I heard the pilot yell out, "Godspeed" and the green light flashed. I propelled myself through the opening and began to scan for the flare.

As I gained speed, positioning my belly toward the earth, I spotted the flare. In this position you are typically falling at roughly 120 mph. This is the usual position you see people in when they are parachuting recreationally. This was not recreational jumping. Our goal was always to minimize time in the air as much as possible so I quickly pointed my head toward the flare, knowing that my top speed would quickly increase to almost 180 mph.

I further streamlined my body, keeping my head toward the target and moving my hands back alongside my body. The alignment was quite similar to ski-jumpers, or ski flyers, as they are referred to now. Subtle changes in the angle of your hands could now adjust your path as terminal speed approached 250 mph. My large pack was slowing me down otherwise I could have gotten to over 300 mph. You could not pull a chute at that speed anyway so when I approached the release altitude I returned to a belly down position, slowing quickly.

I pulled the chute and began to control my speed and direction with the handles hanging on each side of my head. I watched for signs of wind direction, possible enemies on the ground and safest landing options. As I drifted comfortably down towards the flare, I could see there was nothing around. I also saw there was no open landing area.

I would likely get hung up in a tree so needed to be moving as slowly as possible and come in at the right angle to minimize chances of injury.

I pulled down hard on the handles and soon found myself dangling about 15 feet in the air. Rather than a complete cutaway and dropping that distance, I had been trained to cut one side only, release both handles and ride the chute closer to the ground. Keeping a tight grip with my arms and legs I soon found myself only four feet off the ground. I cut the other lines and dropped free.

I quickly grabbed my pistol so I could get to a less obvious spot and upgrade to my automatic rifle. It was basically a modified AR 15. The original AR 15, shooting 5.56 mm rounds can't even take down deer sized game so was never a weapon of choice. Although it is effective up to 250 yards or so and used by many SWAT teams and other law enforcement, it was now out of vogue with the military.

The AR 15 had been around since 1958. SEALs and others favored the FN SCAR Mk16/Mk17 platform. It is very modifiable and fires 5.56 or 7.62 NATO rounds at a rate of up to 625 per minute. More than ten rounds per second! It weighs almost 8 pounds but is my weapon of choice. When I decide I must pull trigger, I want deadly force and I want a lot of it available.

I surveyed the area and found an outcropping of rock that provided me with cover from above and kept my back protected. I moved carefully over the ground, watching for any trip wires, and got to the rocks.

As I confirmed my rifle was prepared, and slipped clips into my vest and pants, I kept my pistol at the ready.

Chapter Twelve – More Training

I had a small ear bud that I was to insert and when I did, I almost immediately heard a male voice. "Welcome to the island", was all he said. I asked where I was to move to, and he said he would send the coordinates directly to my small GPS. He explained that I had no more than one hour to get to that point where I would be met by another operator.

Based on where I was on the GPS display, it appeared I had to travel at least four miles in that time. It was doable, depending of course on what was encountered along the way and the land I had to traverse. It went quickly as I moved over the terrain with relative ease. I was prepared for anything so wasn't exactly racing ahead, I remembered my SEAL training that you never wanted to run to your death. Real or imagined.

I eventually came to the edge of a clearing with the GPS showing my contact point almost directly across from me. I certainly was not going to cross the clearing, so I took the circuitous route and stayed in the bush. As I approached the destination a person stepped out from in front of a tree, extended his hand and simply said, "I'm your contact, please follow me."

Soon we were in a small camouflage covered Quonset hut. As we stepped through the door, I noticed it had a table covered with electronics.

There was also a table on the other side with all kinds of weapons and cots for four people. It appeared we would be roughing it during this training.

He explained that this part of my training would last as long as it had to.

I would be told when I was finished, and he would be my evaluator. He said that I could ask any questions I wanted, but to expect a lot of "no comment" as that was often the case.

What came next was what felt like months of even more challenging training and physical things that rivalled even the SEAL SQT training I had just successfully completed. It was hard to believe there could be anything more challenging than that, but this was it.

Each day and night any number of situations could arise. "Attacks" by two or more hostiles, gun battles, knife fights and individual target packages like what SEALs encountered. I excelled at everything but especially at hand-to-hand combat and weapons. I was a deadly shot, whether in sniper mode, on the move, or even using a pistol. It seemed like I could acquire targets quicker than anyone I had seen thus far. While others may have had similar visual acuity, I was a split second quicker on locking in, determining friend or foe and pulling the trigger.

I chalk up my sniper skills and response time to my Grandfather. He was a very accomplished sniper in WW1. A real gentleman too.

These were all semi-live ammo events. The shells behaved exactly like regular 5.56 rounds but did not fire a standard projectile. They were like laser tag fights in that if you were hit your ear bud told you where and how bad. You then had to react to your situation.

While I was highly skilled in all the weapon aspects, I really loved any and all hand to hand. I was unsure if I was getting "special" treatment because I was female or not, but it felt like these guys were putting a little extra into everything. Rather than make it easier on me, what had been typical so far was that I was pushed harder.

I had no idea who they were, where they came from or what would happen next, so I had to prepare for anything. At least in SQT there was some semblance of order, this was more chaotic. Much more!

On any given day, I could be thrust into multiple life-threatening situations. It seemed like every second or third day I would be given a profile of an individual and sent into the bush to track them, subdue them, and move on to another target.

The training was relentless. Day after day, each day more challenging than the one before. Soon, I was almost the perfect fighting machine. I had faced and defeated two and sometime three men at once. I did not come out completely unscathed, but I always came out the winner.

I typically hit the rack and slept very soundly, except for the fact that my mind was always on high alert. I could be in the middle of a sound sleep, hear a slight noise anywhere around me and be immediately ready to go.

I was the definition of a hair trigger at that point.

It was during one of these events that I was told my training was complete. I had done everything expected of me and more, I was leaving the next day. It felt surreal to me that I had again succeeded.

I always believed in my own ability and skill, but this training was a lot different than any other. There is a lot that went on which I can never divulge to anyone, nor would I wish to. Suffice to say, I was extremely pleased to be finished.

Chapter Thirteen – My First Target Package

I left before sunrise the next day; coordinates sent to my GPS watch. I moved slowly through the jungle-like brush, carrying my full pack. I was on medium alert as even though my training was complete you could never be certain. Shortly after I arrived at my exfil point I heard the rotors of a helo and watched as a line dropped down.

I heard a voice in my ear bud as Cato told me to get up that line and don't waste any time. Scrambling up a line dangling from a helo and carrying a full pack on your back is not easy. I moved quickly up the line though, thankful for the knots each 24 inches that I could use both hands and feet on. I was pulled inside just as the helo banked sharply left and sped off.

Cato congratulated me on my training, telling me I was the most impressive candidate they had seen since this began, more than nine years previous. The helo was blacked out, just like the plane had been so I had no idea where I was nor where I was going. I knew that I would find out soon enough.

We chatted while we flew to our next location, Cato letting me know that I was being thrown into the deep end. They knew I could be successful, and they knew the mission I was being given would interest me.

He said we were on our way to an air base where we would board a plane that was taking a SEAL team on a mission. We were going to speak to no one nor interact with the team at all. They had their mission, and I would soon have mine.

We landed at a low-key air base where I spotted a large C-17 cargo aircraft sitting on the tarmac. These were serious flying machines capable of carrying 102 troops, Humvees and even tanks. With a range of more than 7,000 miles and a top speed of almost 600 mph, these things did all the heavy lifting. They could be found almost anywhere in the world.

I was aware that a heavily modified version of the C-17 was often used to transport SEAL teams and all their gear. They can even maintain a base of operations in the air or on the ground. Cato told me to get ready to leave as the SEALs were being spun-up now and they always leave on time.

Being "spun up" is a take on the spinning rotor blades of a helo and signifies the SEAL team is going into action. Cato and I had a separate section where the two of us sat with a small table, a couple of gear lockers and two hammock-style bunks. I watched out of the corner of my eye as the SEALs began to board and go to their section. I didn't recognize anyone but that made sense as it was unlikely there would be anyone from my SQT training class that would be on a mission yet.

Finally, we began to rumble along the tarmac and slowly lift into the air. Cato and I sat down, and he slid two file folders across the table to me. He asked if I knew who Stephen Mills was. I said of course I did and said that I have his name on my knife. I said how disgusted I was that so many men died that day on Extortion-17.

Cato smiled and said that was good, connection to the mission was always critical.

My target package contained a great deal of information including a photo of an Afghani male. He told me that they had confirmed, thanks to bragging amongst his friends, that this person is the one who fired the RPG at the helo that fateful day. He was my HVT, High Value Target. So, I would be getting revenge for the man whose name I carried on my Ka-Bar knife. A fallen SEAL. A dead brother.

I knew that Kabul was more than 7,300 miles from US soil, so this was going to be roughly a 15-hour flight. We would likely require in-air refueling which would slow us down a bit too. As we reviewed details, last known location of the target, and everything else, Cato said it would be a HALO entry. HALO stands for High Altitude, Low Opening in the parachute world.

I would be cutting through the sky like a dagger toward my landing target at a speed approaching 300 miles per hour. When I reached the lowest possible point at which I could open my chute I would do so and hopefully land in one piece. My goggles contained a small heads-up display that provided me with a cross hair target to aim myself at. It even included corrections for wind speed, terrain, and curve of the earth. It was a little like a video game except for the fact it really was life or death!

We reviewed locations over and over, terrain challenges, and what to watch for. Thanks to my darker complexion I would resemble an afghani woman and with a head scarf on I could move around relatively freely if it was required. I knew however, that I would travel mostly at night and would not likely be without my ruck and weapons. I even had a garrotte balled up in my top pocket so I could get at it quickly.

I was able to sleep for a couple of hours to ensure I was rested when I jumped. I knew the time was close so I began to check and re-check my gear, weapons, maps, and everything else I would need. I had an earwig for communication and a spare one just in case. Cato said that there would be an overwatch person using a silent drone to help guide me and warn me of problems.

Soon the time was at hand. I was ready to go. Oddly, I had little fear that I was being dropped close to Peshawar in Pakistan. I would then have to make my way over some rough terrain to Jalalabad, where the target was most recently seen. He had been seen outside the city in a place called Kameh. It was close to a river and there was a possibility I could use that same river to get there once I passed Torkham, which was close to the border.

The rear bay opened, I confirmed all my gear was good to go, put on my oxygen mask and helmet and jumped when Cato tapped me on the shoulder. I pointed my head down, put my hands at my side and felt my speed continue to increase. I was going straight at the cross hairs in my goggles and now travelling close to 280 mph.

As I approached my open point, I oriented myself back to belly towards earth and slowed down to a speed at which I could safely open my chute. When I saw the altimeter approaching the setpoint I pulled and watched as my canopy deployed. Soon I was guiding myself towards the cross hairs and in no time landed softly as I pulled down hard on the control cables.

I quickly released the chute, balled it up as tightly as I could and stashed it under a tree and some rocks. I ensured everything was as it was when I jumped and listened for contact. I was being monitored closely by my overwatch person and soon heard a female voice. She said she would be my eyes in the sky and then said, "let's go get this bastard."

I moved at a reasonable pace off to the side of a road. We had already determined that river access would not be possible. I was told that I was approaching a gathering of three small dwellings directly ahead and I would be met by a man called Firash. I moved cautiously through the brush until I saw a lone figure ahead. He was standing next to a dirty-looking farm truck.

I approached from his back, first leaving time to ensure there was nobody else close by. The voice in my ear said they were all friendlies, there was no one else around and she would tell me if any showed. We had not yet met face to face, but she said I needed to trust her, we were a team.

I popped up on the other side of the truck box, my pistol trained on him, and asked if he was Firash. He turned and smiled and said we needed to get moving quickly as my target had been located. They were unsure how long he would be at one location, so we had to move.

I stashed my ruck and gear in a cubby hidden behind a false bottom in the truck. I had my Berettas with me, my WASP knife stuck in one boot, a standard Ka-Bar knife in the other boot and the makings of a garrotte in my pocket. I was practically a walking armory.

Firash provided me with a bunch of local clothing, including a head scarf, and we left about ten minutes after I arrived. Soon we were rumbling down the road like any other couple might be.

The man driving, the woman sitting patiently at his side. The whole ride Firash was talking to me about the region, the people, how men acted and how women acted. It was all information I knew already, but the refresh helped quite a bit.

We had been driving for close to an hour when Firash said we were getting close to the point where I would have to go on alone. He pulled over, we nodded and off I went. I trekked through the brush, paralleling the road just far enough away to remain unseen. My earwig crackled to life, and I heard that familiar voice. She said I had about seven miles to navigate and would need to be very aware of my surroundings.

As I was approaching a rise in the land, she said there were two people over to the right about a hundred yards out. She was using heat detecting equipment so the shapes were displayed to her as bodies, but I knew from training that was all the detail she would see. I grabbed one of my Berettas, checked the clip and slipped the safety off. I tucked it back into my belt and constantly scanned the area as I moved cautiously forward.

I chose to avoid them so travelled a little further to go around. They would never see or hear me at that distance and soon I was past them.

I continued moving quickly over the terrain, the only sounds the crunching of my boots on the hardpan and the voice in my ear telling me to continue as I was. It was warm and I was glad I had already stashed my ruck.

Chapter Fourteen - Capture

As I continued moving ahead. I heard my contact start to say something but then hit a dead spot and her voice cut out. Overwatch was great but I was always vigilant anyway. I used my GPS to keep headed toward my target.

That was when it happened. A mere momentary lack of focus, as I checked my GPS, and I was hit by something. It wasn't a bullet as I heard nothing but had the wind knocked out of me and I fell to the ground. As I regained my senses I was already tied up and being dragged behind two men.

They could be anyone, it was difficult to tell in this area. Afghani rebels, Afghan soldiers, non-military, there were many possibilities. I knew I had been searched and most, if not all, of my weapons were now in their possession. They took me into a small metal shed and lashed me to a chair. I had no idea what was about to happen but knew that I would most certainly need to get myself out of here sooner rather than later.

One of them stood in front of me and asked where I came from. Are you American? I hadn't even finished shaking my head no when the back of his hand cracked across my face. He hit me so hard he almost knocked me and the chair completely over. Inside my head I smiled as I imagined what I would do to this pig when I got my chance.

Based on the way I was tied and the fact I was tied with ropes and not plastic zip ties I felt these clowns were amateurs. I also knew that if I did not escape quickly this could still end poorly for me.

I endured the yelling, slaps to the face and blows to the head as I bided my time. I was already in the zone where my thoughts and mind were elsewhere. This enabled me to plan while absorbing the punishment. Soon, one of them finally left the room and I was left with only one.

The next question he asked I whispered my answer as quietly as I could. I told him I would talk but I needed some water, my throat was too dry to speak. I had already freed my hands although I kept them behind my back, hoping he would suspect nothing.

I was pleased to see him go to a table and grab a canteen. I wasn't about to drink anything they gave me but thankfully he came close. He grabbed my face and squeezed my mouth open. As he was raising the canteen I lunged forward and up, driving my head straight up into his eye socket.

I had no need to find out who these idiots were, nor did I need any information from them. Before he could yell or call out to his buddy, I struck him hard up into the nose.

I felt the bones shatter and knew he was already close to dead. I spun him around and locked in a choke on him. I slipped my off hand around to the side of his head, twisted quickly and snapped his neck.

His partner could return at any time, so I needed to move him out of eyesight and get back into my chair. I drug him behind a table and scrambled back. Just as I sat down and wrapped the ropes around my legs and got my hands behind the chair the other guy entered the shed.

He glanced around and then was also stupid enough to get too close to me. I didn't know if there were more men outside, but I had to take this opportunity. He came within arms reach. In one motion I stood and delivered a vicious kick to his groin. I was certain he was permanently altered as he collapsed in pain.

It mattered not as I wasn't about to let him live either. He tried to stand up and as he did, I delivered a roundhouse kick to his head that most likely destroyed his jaw. I grabbed him up and choked the life out of him too as he kicked his feet wildly. I dropped him to the ground, looked around for any weapons I could get and went to the front of the shed.

I heard nothing nor did I see anything. As I stuck my head out, I could hear the voice in my ear once again. She said we had lost contact, but she could see there were two people. I had no way to speak back so simply waited for her next words. She said there was nobody else around.

I scouted around and found my pistols, knives and garotte. I felt whole again knowing that I had what were now the tools of my trade.

Chapter Fifteen – Back On Track

I composed myself and moved back out in into the woods. My overwatch sent the new coordinates to my watch, and I followed it for about an hour. I was told the target had been spotted again. He appeared to be encamped just outside Kameh. That meant he had been there for a few days at least, perhaps travelling between two locations. I was hoping it may be his home and not a well armed base or training camp for the rebels.

Now that I was getting closer, I began to fully appreciate the gravity of what I was about to do. This bastard killed our brave men and women. Extortion 17 had no reason to believe the enemy had an RPG capable of taking out a well-armed helo. But they did, and I was going to exact revenge. I hoped I would be able to isolate him so I could punish him and make him understand exactly why he was about to die.

I moved stealthily over the ground, hyper-vigilant to everything around me. I had to move more slowly as I approached the encampment. It appeared to me that this may indeed be his home. Perhaps he was on a little R&R, completely unsuspecting of what was coming his way? I waited for the voice in my ear to tell me how many there were and how close any other locations or people were. This would give me an indication of how much time I would have after the initial assault.

Soon, I could see a small structure. No, two. My overwatch told me there were three heat signatures and they were all in one building. I had the image of this guy's face burned into my mind.

I hunkered down and concealed myself as I waited. I hoped one would come out for any reason, so I could eliminate him. Minutes later a young boy emerged. Damn it, I wasn't going to take out a child. This wasn't about atrocity; it was about payback. Our enemies might make him watch as they killed an American demon, an infidel. That was not what we did, now or ever.

The young boy seemed to be just playing outside. He was gathering up some sticks, most likely for a fire. I watched and waited, hoping he would come close. I knew what I was about to do was both dangerous and risky, but I felt I had no choice. He got close enough for me to grab him and cover his mouth as I did so.

I quickly gagged him and carried him away from the structure so I could tie him to a tree. Once he was securely tied up and incapable of making any noise I returned to my spot. I heard a female voice call out from the structure and shortly after, the door opened. She came out and looked around.

When she went to check the other structure, I was able to grab her as well and gag her. She appeared to be completely non-military. I immediately decided I would secure her the same way I did the son.

I knew that what I was doing would certainly make my escape more dangerous, but I had no intention of killing innocents.

Chapter Sixteen – The Ultimate Revenge

I moved quietly over the ground and crouched low, next to the door. Whether he came out with a weapon or not I would be ready. It took longer than expected and then I heard overwatch tell me he was on the move.

The door across from me swung open and as he stepped out, I connected with a hard strike to his jaw, knocking him back into the building. He had no gun and no knife so I knew this would not end well for this coward. I circled as he planned his move. He came straight at me, and I slipped his pathetic attempt at punching me and connected hard with his throat.

He fell quickly and in seconds I had him zip-tied to a chair. I pulled up another chair and sat across from him. I told him I knew he spoke English so I would make this easy on him. I looked into his scared eyes and told him I was about to send him to hell.

I asked him if he recalled what happened August 6th of 2011? Clearly, he knew as his eyes widened. He composed himself and said he had shot down the infidels who were trying to kill his people. As the last word came out of his mouth, I delivered a straight shot and exploded his nose. There was blood everywhere and he spat at me and said his work was done.

I wanted to scare him a bit. Even though I had no intention of torturing this guy I wanted him to worry about it. The same way my brothers in arms must have worried as that helo plummeted from the sky. My package had contained photos not only of him but of his family. I dangled each photo in front of his face.

I explained in detail the pain I would inflict on each as I held the photos close to him. I watched his eyes get darker and soon he was telling me his own comrades would track me down. I smiled and said that was highly unlikely. I got to him easily, didn't I? I pointed out the dangerous regions I was able to traverse.

Of course, I had absolutely no intention of hurting his wife or child, that was not who I was. They may have supported him and hated Americans too but that was no reason to hurt them. I needed him to feel the helplessness, the resignation that my brothers must have felt as they plunged to their death. I looked into his eyes and knew it was time.

Much as I would have preferred a fight to the death, as one sided as it would have been, I left him tied to the chair. I prepared my garrotte as I moved around behind him. I made the loop, dropped it over his head and began to pull as it settled on his neck. He tried to kick and struggle as I slowly tightened the loop of wire.

It was only beginning to cut the skin as I had not yet exerted full pressure. He was coughing and sputtering as he struggled to breathe. I wanted him to experience a little more pain, so I left him squirming for another minute until I pulled the loop tighter. The razor-sharp wire easily cut deeper into the skin, blood now running freely down his chest.

I pulled each handle outward with all my strength and that was it. He was gone, a soon-to-be glaring example of what happens when you screw with the USA. Zip tied to a chair, an ever-expanding pool of blood gathering at his feet.

I took a couple of photos, gathered myself and walked out the front door. Overwatch let me know there were no other bodies anywhere close except for the two I knew about.

I left my balaclava on and went to the boy and the woman. I left them tightly tied but freed one hand so they could drink the water I was leaving for them. I knew they would be found, likely too soon for me, but just soon enough for them.

Chapter Seventeen – Get Me Out of Here

I moved quickly away from the site, needing to put serious distance between me and them. If they were found sooner, I knew there would be an all-out manhunt. I wrestled with the idea of not retrieving my pack but decided I felt safer having all my weapons with me. I would use the element of surprise to keep me moving forward.

The voice in my ear came to life again and told me the GPS coordinates were now on my watch. I was headed to Kabul. I was then told I had to go to Jalalabad first. I would be meeting a contact who would take me to the airport after providing me with all the clothing and cover documents I would need. I was shocked they would take such a brazen approach, but I had no choice except to get on board with the plan.

As I moved through the brush, she told me they would never look for someone to use the airport. My contact person was a man named Aimal and we would pose as husband and wife. I continued moving as quickly as was safe and soon my GPS indicated I was within 500 yards of the planned meet. I took up a position that was well protected but allowed me to see almost 360 degrees of the surrounding area.

I watched a tall, dark man walk out into the small opening and the voice in my ear told me that was Aimal. I emerged from my cover to greet him. We shook hands and he smiled saying he was glad I had made it. He took me to his home where I was given luggage, papers, and all the travelling clothing I would need.

Our back story was complete and comprehensive. There were few details to focus on, and if anything else outside of those came up, I was to follow his lead. It was normal for the man to do all the talking anyway, even at airport security, so that would not raise any red flags. He got us some food and we ate quietly.

It was all very tasty, traditional Afghan food. He told me about our meal which included Pulao which was steamed rice with raisins and carrots and mantu. Mantu are meat filled dumplings steamed and topped with a yogurt sauce that had lemon, garlic, and mint in it. I could also taste cardamom, turmeric and saffron, all typical in Afghan cooking. I ate well and was thankful there was plenty.

Of course, there was no liquor at all. Even an operative contact like him would not risk the punishment for locals consuming alcoholic beverages of any sort. One could be imprisoned or get 60 lashes with a whip. Sharia law was nothing to toy with.

As we sat, he explained we would be flying via Turkish airlines and headed to Canada. We would eventually land in Halifax, a city on the far Eastern coast of the country. It is situated above Maine. There would be a few stops, the penultimate one being in Montreal. I knew of Montreal as a party city, and it was also rumored to be a bit of a haven for terrorists.

He said it would be the perfect cover as, thanks to Liberal governments, there was a great deal of immigration encouraged. People of every color and race easily blended within the population.

A stopover in Montreal might also allow us to simply disappear if that was required. We made our way to the airport the next day and, other than heavily armed guards everywhere, I was surprised at how smoothly it went.

I asked him if I would see my ruck again? Aimal said he had a partner who was taking my pack and weapons so that it could be flown home to me. Leaving weapons behind was never a good idea. Soon, after a twice over by security and what looked to be army personnel, we boarded our flight. I was calmer once we were in the air, but we had to retain our covers as you never knew who was on a flight like this.

I slept soundly until we landed in Istanbul where we had to change planes. We gathered our luggage and cooled our jets in the airport as we waited the 2 hours and 50 minutes for our next flight to Montreal.

We drank some strong Turkish coffee, that was quite tasty, as we sat quietly doing our best to attract no attention.

I had a sense of relief wash over me when we were seated on the next aircraft. Finally, the doors closed, and we rumbled down the runway and eased into the air. Next stop Montreal, Canada. I read up a little more about it on the plane and it sounded interesting, but I was hoping we would still go to our ticketed final destination, Halifax.

We had a long layover in Montreal, more than twelve hours and when we landed Aimal said we should take a tour. Although we would have to clear security again it would be easier and less risky than hanging around the airport. That is exactly what we did.

Aimal knew Montreal and it was a glorious sunny and clear day. He got us a car and driver and off we went. I've always been a total tourist, so this was right up my alley.

I found out Montreal was an island and lived with two official languages, English, and French. Of course, I knew Spanish very well so French really wasn't much of a leap and I had found it easy to learn at Georgetown. If you know one romance language you can get along in any of the others.

We were both hungry and Aimal told the driver to take us to a small restaurant he knew of. It was owned and operated by Jewish people. He said we would be having bagels with lox, capers, and cream cheese. Lox was a typical Jewish food that most people think is smoked salmon. Lox is salmon, but it was originally cured in a brine and not smoked. Nowadays it is lightly salted and cold smoked and the terms LOX and smoked salmon have come to mean the same thing. I fell in love on my first bite. Call it whatever you like it was tasty.

We had a great tour of the city as we talked about his life in Afghanistan, including the loss of his family. He said that soon after that happened, he decided he would help the Americans. I was glad he did as I knew that I was in good hands. I still marvel at how easily I got out of that country.

We spoke again about disappearing in Montreal, but we agreed that completing the flight would be much safer. Flight records were shared with many levels of government, police, and military. We wanted to ensure that we drew no attention to ourselves for any reason.

The rest of the day was enjoyable. I got to see many of the sights in Montreal including the site of the 1967 World's Fair. It was called Man and His World, and it was on a small island adjacent to Montreal. There are only a few buildings left now, one of which is a casino.

Sooner than expected, we were headed back to the airport and clearing security one more time. We had already cleared customs when we landed in Montreal, so this was just standard, domestic flight security on our way out.

Chapter Eighteen – Halifax, Canada

After a short flight we deplaned in Halifax and decided at that point we would go our separate ways. I was flying solo anyway, no earwig, no support but that was no big deal for me. The airport was called Stanfield International and, me being me, I wanted to know who that was.

Robert Stanfield was Canada's version of a state governor in that he was the Premier of Nova Scotia a long time ago. Apparently, he came the closest of any previous Premier to becoming Canada's President (known as a Prime Minister) in the seventies. He has been referred to as the best Prime Minister Canada NEVER had and he has quite the record as a Premier.

I have always been a tourist extraordinaire, and this trip would be no exception. I had plenty of cash and time on my hands as I had not been contacted in any way by Cato or anyone else. I had numerous email accounts that I could check from anywhere so I would know if I was needed. They were virtually impossible to track or find and we dealt in code when we spoke anyway, so it was completely safe.

I got myself a rental car, with GPS, and plugged in the hotel I decided to stay at.

It was called the Lord Nelson and it was close to the heart of downtown Halifax. I parked, checked into my room, and went upstairs to relax. It was what one might call a stately older hotel.

Even though it had been renovated it wasn't exactly five-star, but that suited me fine. It had lots of character and I liked that.

The Lord Nelson was one of the few buildings left standing after the huge Halifax explosion during WW 1. The "Halifax Explosion" was a massive blast that is memorialized in various spots around the city.

In December of 1917 a French cargo ship called the SS Mont-Blanc was transporting high explosives from New York City to Bordeaux, France via Halifax. There had been a large British offensive at Cambrai, France that was the first large scale use of tanks in war. They needed to replace fuel and, most importantly, ordnance to continue the fight.

As the Mont-Blanc steamed slowly (roughly one knot) through the narrows of the harbor it was stuck by an unladen Norwegian vessel called the SS IMO. The Mont-Blanc had stored many barrels of benzol on the deck.

Due to its propensity to ooze explosive vapors, this was deemed the safest place to store it. It was these fumes that were ignited by sparks from the low-speed collision and soon the whole ship was ablaze.

They fought as best they could but before long the fire was out of control. About twenty minutes after it first caught fire, the Mont-Blanc exploded. It was the largest man-made explosion of the time with energy approaching 2.9 kilotons of TNT.

It ripped through the port and the surrounding cityscape like a hurricane.

Buildings within a half mile radius were obliterated. Metal poles and structures bent like plastic drinking straws from the blast pressure. Over 2,000 people died and more than 9,000 were injured. The photos I saw clearly showed the devastation, loss of life, and extensive damage that almost levelled the entire city.

After reading this little bit of history, I wanted to see that harbor up close. I must have dozed off as I awoke with the book spread across my chest and the sun beating down on me through the window of my room. It was a beautiful sunny day and, this being a seaport, it had a certain vibe to it. It was sort of like a little San Francisco as downtown was very hilly.

I decided I needed a run. I stretched out a bit and got into my running gear and took off.

I was headed nowhere in particular but knowing I was after about a six-mile run, or ten kilometres, as they say in Canada. I found that whole metric thing interesting. It always intrigued me that almost the whole rest of the world, including our next-door neighbor, uses metric but the states never did adopt it. I think we just don't deal with change all that well. That and metric wasn't an American invention.

I spoke briefly to the doorman to get directions to the waterfront and off I went. Soon, I was pounding along a beautiful wooden boardwalk next to the ocean. In my own little world, I enjoyed the sun warming my face as the cooler breeze came in off the harbor. I could not believe this place was not wall to wall people. I looked around constantly as I ran and really liked what I saw.

The harbor was clean and smooth. I could even see some small Navy ships off in the distance towards the top of the harbor. I knew a little about the Canadian Navy. It had quickly become the third largest navy in the world during WW 2.

Of course, the bulk of those "ships" were tiny Corvettes and Frigates, but they were still ocean-going ships. Certainly not ships I would choose to be on in that part of the Atlantic, but plenty of Canadian sailors served on them. They protected convoys heading to England with supplies and ferrying troops back and forth.

They were especially careful of the German U-boats, which were very deadly at the time. They had primitive sonar to try to track them and used depth charges to blow them out of the water or at least damage them when they could locate them. There was even one of those Corvettes down on the waterfront and I decided after my run and cool down I wanted to have a look. I had never been on a Canadian warship.

I ran past a cruise ship terminal and a smaller container terminal and suddenly found myself in a large park. It was only five minutes away from downtown, but I felt like I was running in the woods. Point Pleasant Park was a great place to run. It had historical war memorials all over the place. It was clear this was an ideal place from which to defend the Halifax harbor and I knew there must be thousands of stories about this land.

I had a great run around and through the park and planned my six miles to end back at the boardwalk. I got there after passing the cruise ship terminal once more and stretched out on the grass and did a little light yoga, while gazing into the harbor.

When I finished and had cooled down sufficiently, I walked back down the boardwalk to the HMCS Sackville.

I decided to take the guided tour. It was even smaller up close it seemed. I would find out that this was the last of Canada's 123 Corvettes. It is the only one of the 269 allied corvettes from the second world war that remains. They seem very tiny to exist in the frigid North Atlantic.

They are only about two hundred feet long and have a displacement of a mere 950 tons. It was powered by one 4-cylinder steam engine that produced 2,750 HP. That seemed like a lot of horsepower for four cylinders to me.

The tour really brought the trials and tribulations these sailors faced into focus for me. I felt very cramped and had to duck often while walking about the ship. I imagined how many sailors likely cracked their head open on those low bulkheads. I would not even fit in the bunks that were no more than hammocks strung from the superstructure.

The cadet leading the tour was excellent. He went into great detail and was clearly very proud of his grandfather, who had served on one of these. The Sackville had a great story and people loved telling it.

It is a floating museum, moored at its harbor location in spring, summer and early fall. I completed the tour and felt like I had learned a lot about Canada, and its navy, in a very short time.

I strolled leisurely back to the hotel and decided I would take a long drive the next day. The concierge told me the Cabot Trail was world famous and once I drove it, I could clearly see why. The Cabot Trail is recognized as one of the World's most scenic destinations and was named after the Italian explorer John Cabot. He real name was actually Giovanni Caboto but, like many others, his name was anglicized. He landed somewhere in that area in 1497.

It was an amazing day driving around that trail, going from seaside to highlands and back to seaside. It was like three completely different worlds. I decided this would not be the last time I visit this part of our continent.

When I returned to the hotel, I decided to go home the next day. I felt I had seen enough for now and needed to ground myself once more.

Chapter Nineteen – Heading Home

I felt like taking a bus or train if I could, so I began doing the research. Unfortunately, there didn't appear to be an easy way to make such a trip. I could have gotten to New York, but my favorite Aunt lived close to Portland, Maine and I really wanted to see her. We had always kept in close contact and while I could not reveal what I was doing I was excited to see her and speak to her again.

I had spent many a great week visiting with her at her home in Old Orchard Beach, about 20 miles South of Portland. It was situated about halfway between Portland and Kennebunkport, a famous Presidential vacation spot. I never quite understood why you would need a "vacation" away from Hyannis Port but what did I know. George H.W. Bush (number 41) is the most famous resident of Kennebunkport at Walker's Point. My aunt always spoke tirelessly of the history of the area, and I was always willing to listen and learn.

I was able to get a flight close to noon the following day and found myself deplaning at the Portland International Jetport late in the afternoon. I had sent my aunt a note and told her I would be at her house around dinnertime. I wanted to take us out to dinner, but she quickly responded that I would do no such thing.

She was quite the culinary talent and could prepare almost any style of meal to perfection. As I stepped out of the car in her driveway, I could already smell the food cooking. I walked up the pathway, her door flew open, and she ran out to greet me, giving me a huge hug.

We ate well and chatted deep into the night. We hung around the next day too and that was when she told me that when she was "gone" I was going to inherit everything, including her house in Southern California. I explained she didn't have to do that and why wouldn't she leave it to her remaining sister or their kids or something?

She said that I was the one she felt the most connected to and that she believed I would do great things with my life. She went on to explain that often doing great things does not bring great wealth and she wanted me to not have to worry about money. She wanted me to fully enjoy everything life had to offer. I felt badly that I couldn't reveal how tenuous my hold on life might be, knowing the type of work I would be doing, but I could say nothing.

We ended up back at her house close to sunset and again stayed up late talking. She said she would soon be out at her California house for at least three months and made me promise to visit her there. We agreed and I slept very well that night. There was a tearful goodbye in the morning as I left for the airport. I was soon winging my way back to California.

Lake Michigan was also a beautiful place, but I wanted to get as far away from that camp as I could. Soon I was emerging from the terminal at LAX, the Southern California sun warming my face.

As I waited for a taxi, I noticed two or three people, who I assumed were vets, each with dogs. I sat next to one and found out that it wasn't him who needed "comforting", they had placed the dog with him, on the dogs' behalf. He was a very inquisitive and friendly Belgian

Malinois. That was the new German Shepherd as far as the army was concerned.

I couldn't help but think "small world" when he went on to explain the dog had been with a SEAL team. They could only operate for a short period of time, and they had a re-homing project active for them. The dogs were typically matched with vets who required a support animal. In this case the man was simply a dog lover, who was also a vet, who knew he could take care of this four-legged patriot for the rest of his days.

The dog was very clearly dedicated to the man, never taking his eyes off him. The man was similarly connected to the dog, meeting his gaze with a look of admiration. It was heart warming to see, and I decided right then and there, once I was off active duty, I would get myself a dog. I wanted that feeling.

Finally, my taxi arrived and in no time, I was back in my apartment. I slept and calmed down for two days before I decided to head over to my gym.

Chapter 20 - Downtime

The only thing that Cato had said to me after my mission was that I should first rest and then get back to training. There was nothing said about my next assignment, only that it was likely four to six months away.

I grabbed my bag and headed to the gym. This was really the place I felt most at home on this earth. I warmed up while taking in the surroundings and evaluating who was in the gym with me. I saw the usual people one would expect at a gym like this one close to Los Angeles.

A couple of steroid monkeys complete with cartoon-like large muscles but very little real strength.One or two barbie doll types dressed to the nines and seemingly there more to attract glances from men, or women I suppose, than to train hard.

A few committed males and females who were working as hard as they thought they could. Of course, they didn't know what I knew. Training only until you feel like you cannot go further or heavier rather than busting through that minor pause to push yourself higher and higher.

A couple of the girls stood out though. They were doing their own thing, spotting each other, and training reasonably hard. At least for what I was sure was considered hard by a couple of realtors, or whatever they did for a living. That was when I spotted Hector. He was at another level above everyone else in that gym.

He was clearly a finely tuned machine. I caught glimpses of him out of the corner of my eye, lifting heavy and with great control. He paused to stretch every now and then and you could see that sinewy muscles made up a large percentage of his body weight. This was no steroid junkie, and he certainly didn't seem to care about anything else that was going on around him. He was focused and blissfully oblivious to his surroundings.

We seemed to be doing a similar routine so ended up overlapping on the odd piece of equipment. I began to work up to my typical squat weight and noticed him standing there. He smiled and said it was good to see someone else training the way he did. I glanced around the gym, smiled back, and said there didn't seem to be too many of us here today. He chuckled and introduced himself. I shook his hand, told him my name, and went back to work.

We ended up completing our workouts at roughly the same time and he asked how things went. We just kept chatting and we discovered we both had interest in martial arts.

He seemed impressed when I told him I was a Judoka and which level I was at. I also told him I really enjoyed Brazilian Jiu-jitsu and other hand to hand combat techniques.

We saw each other at the gym often after that first meeting. The usual head nods and smiles between two almost-acquaintances. Hector and

I ended up hanging out together often and it made waiting for my next mission not quite so tedious.

Chapter 20 One – Hanging with Hector

Hector and I spent more and more time together as I settled back into a normal life. Of course, what was "normal" for me now? I really couldn't say. Along that line, I was beginning to wonder if I would ever have PTSD. It seemed many soldiers and others did these days. I decided I should keep a close eye on myself and make sure I watched for any signs.

I really enjoyed training with Hector. While he wasn't my equal, he was close in a couple of disciplines. We were almost equal in Brazilian Jiu-Jitsu so that was a big help to me. We sparred often after training in the gym, and I really enjoyed it. It was after one of these sessions where I got into a bit of trouble.

I left the gym went home and then decided I needed to find a bank close-by so I could get some cash. It was a nice night so I thought I would take a light jog to find one. I tucked my bank card into my inner pocket and went on my way. It wasn't a training run at all, really it was my version of a nice walk.

After a few blocks I spotted a branch so headed to it to get my cash. I inserted my card, got what I wanted and then tucked the bills into my pocket with my card. I felt like wandering around a bit so that's what I did.

There were a few people out and about but not many, so it was easy for me to notice that I was possibly being followed. I took a circuitous route towards home and when it became apparent, they were still following me, I decided to act.

I turned into an alley and wasn't completely surprised when they dropped in right behind me. They closed the gap and then I turned toward them. One told me they wouldn't hurt me if I gave them the cash. I was still hoping to avoid trouble, so I tried to reason with them. I said that I was trained in many fighting styles and, even if they had knives, they were unlikely to be able to beat me. So, no, they weren't going to get my money.

The larger of the two came toward me as he pulled a knife from his jacket. I just smiled at him and asked him once more not to do it. He yelled a couple of not-so-nice things at me and suddenly I saw red. I let him get even closer, the other one not too far behind. When he was close enough, I delivered a hard kick to the outside of his knee. He went down screaming as his leg collapsed.

The knife had flown over into some garbage bags. I let him get to his feet as he began swearing how he was going to kill me. I smiled, said not tonight, and unleashed a strike directly into the center of his chest.

I heard the wind whoosh out of him as he fell and the other one was on me right away. He had no knife so I knew this would be easy.

I felt like having a little fun, so I began to use him like a punching bag. I kept the blows light as I wanted to send a message and hopefully not kill him. I hit him with shot after shot, opening cuts around both eyes and bloodying his nose while he never landed one punch on me.

I knew when he reached inside his jacket that playtime was over. I didn't know if he had a gun or a knife, but I had no intention of finding out. I delivered a roundhouse kick to his head and that was it. They were both down and out. I gathered myself, checked for my cash and card and walked calmly out of the alley towards home.

As I walked in the warm night air, I wondered why I did what I just did. I could have simply avoided it altogether by losing them. Why did I decide that I had to have an actual fight? It was something I needed to consider further and be wary of in the future.

I couldn't risk getting into legal trouble as my handler would be unable to help if it was of a personal nature. I got the sense that if anything did happen to me in civilian life they would simply disappear.

I wasn't too worried as I had kept photocopies of everything I could. Perhaps I could say the trouble was mission-connected.

Chapter 20 Two – The Firepit

In addition to working out and sparring, Hector and I both shared a love for motorcycles. We enjoyed just heading out for rides and we were both Harley enthusiasts. Our rides were both on the louder side but just on the edge of illegal for California. We knew we couldn't pound on the throttles going uphill if there was a noise cop on the rise, but other than that we were good.

It was after one of these rides that we met a couple of Hector's neighbors. It was maybe 11:00 PM and we were moving at not much above an idle. I mean, you could hear our bikes but it's not like they were screaming loud.

As we pulled onto the driveway, we noticed a guy drive his car in right behind us. We got off our bikes, took off our helmets and turned towards him. He got out of his little car yelling at us and Hector told him to just calm down and asked what the problem was. He looked at us and said you and that bitch keep waking up the neighborhood with those damn bikes. Hector said it wasn't us, we barely rode during the week and always tried to keep quiet.

He came toward us, and Hector told him to get back in his car before he let me kick his ass. The guy laughed but stopped when I moved toward him.

He seemed to realize this wasn't a good idea when he saw both of us closer, with our jackets off. He got back into his car, mumbling something about this isn't over. We figured it was, so we headed into the yard for a couple of beers.

Hector got a fire going for us as, even in California, the air cooled down in the evenings this time of year. He got us a beer each and we put our feet up on the edge of the firepit.

We just sat there chatting about all kinds of stuff for what seemed like hours. Suddenly Hector got to his feet when he heard his gate open. I looked back and heard him say you are trespassing. He told them they should leave now before anyone gets hurt, to a group of four rather large dudes.

As they stepped further into the light of the yard, I could see the guy in front was the one from the driveway earlier. He looked at Hector and said I told you this wasn't over. Hector continued to try to reason with them telling them they could have eight guys and they would still lose.

I suppose insulting them that way wasn't the best approach. I got up to join Hector just as two of them started towards him. They closed ground quickly for big guys, but their momentum was about to be used against them.

The first one lunged and Hector took him down easily on the way by as he struck the second guy square on the nose. He was instantly a mess, a real bleeder it seemed. The guy on the ground was about to get up when Hector grabbed his arm and twisted hard in an up and back motion.

I could tell from his yelp and way he looked that his shoulder was completely dislocated, and his arm may even have been broken.

Hector looked at the other two, chuckled and pointed at me telling them if they still want to go, they should take it up with me. They thought it was some sort of trap, so they approached me cautiously. I watched them both closely, deciding I would take out the larger one first. They spread out a bit, which helped me as I looked to deliver my first shot.

As I struck the first one with two quick blows to the head, staggering him, the other one got behind me and tried to get me in a chokehold. Pretty dumb thing to do on his part as Hector had already subdued the other two so could easily get him off me.

I waved Hector off as I drove the heel of my boot as hard as possible onto his instep. His grip weakened as the pain hit him and I spun, while remaining close, and drove my fist up into his abdomen.

I felt his stinky breath hit me as all the air was knocked out of his lungs. As he was falling, I decided I was done and kneed him squarely in the face on his way down. That was it for him.

Now there were four of them on the ground in varying states of consciousness with multiple injuries. Hector stood over them and said they should leave now and if they ever came back, they would be leaving in body bags. They said nothing but I sensed they wouldn't be back.

Hector got a couple more beers, we put our feet back up and all I said was, nice neighborhood you've got here. We laughed and exchanged stories for the rest of the night.

Hector was definitely my kind of guy, a real good friend. He was also obviously the guy you wanted next to you if you were ever in a bar brawl!

Chapter 20 Three – Finally, My Next Mission

After a couple more months of training and general hanging around I was getting restless. I was wondering how long it would be until my next mission. I mean the money was rolling in and I was eating up time, but I wanted to be active. I wanted to be doing things, helping my country.

Soon after that I was finally contacted again by Cato. I was anxious to know what my next mission was, so told him I could meet right away. He was over at my apartment within the hour carrying a leather satchel. I let him in, and we went directly to the kitchen table where he began to unload the satchel.

He had many files and as he sorted them, he began to speak about the scourge of the drug cartels in Mexico and what they were doing to the states. He asked what I knew about El Chapo, and I explained not too much, other than knowing he was recently recaptured and unlikely to escape again.

Cato told me that Joaquin Archivaldo Guzman Loera's (El Chapo) right-hand man, and main assassin, was the one who took over.
El Chapo's sons were involved as well but Ismael Zambada Garcia (aka El Mayo) was the true leader. He went on to explain how dangerous he was and that he needed to be eliminated.

Way back in the early 80's El Mayo, once a farmer, began working with the Juarez Cartel. He was born in Los Mochis Mexico and returned there often. That was where he still had family roots plus it remained a stronghold for the cartel.

Cato said it was critical that this kill looked like another cartel hit so that the fights would start, and they would begin to eliminate one another. He provided me with location details, rough schedules, and several photos of Garcia.

I was also given a dossier on Claudia Ochoa Felix. Apparently, she had been the other main assassin in El Chapo's inner circle. She was very attractive which explained how she was dubbed the "Kim Kardashian of organized crime." Cato said he hoped to get them both if I could.

We discussed details further including things like a safe house, weapons stashes, and other information I would need. I had a few passports and connected drivers' licenses, credit cards and other information to ensure I could return home.

It was always a good idea to drive across the border as there would be a record of when you entered the country which made it easier to exit through the regular border crossings later.

Cato finished up after about four hours of briefing and I was left to plan the balance. I was given a location to pick up a nondescript Honda sedan already setup with insurance for Mexico. I would pick the car up on the south side of San Diego, close to where I would exit the Amtrak train.

I would carry everything I needed, except weapons, in a duffel bag and would pose as a nature photographer. That was always a great cover because people never thought twice about wherever you were going.

I had an address of where I would be staying in Los Mochis which is also where my mini armory would be. I was pumped and ready to go and decided I would catch the first train the next morning and get going. From San Diego to Los Mochis was a little over 800 miles so that segment would be a tedious drive. I would take highway 2 through Mexicali down to Hermosillo and eventually into Los Mochis. The only benefit was that the Sonoran area of Mexico can be quite pretty which makes the drive a little less boring.

I slept well, and in the morning arrived early to the train platform. I sat on the train and sipped orange juice as I watched the ocean pass by on my right. It was really a lovely coastline in that part of California. You passed many famous California locations on that train. Places like New port Beach, Laguna Beach, San Clemente and many more.

I soon arrived at the station, next to old town San Diego, and walked to the address where the car was stored. I punched in the code on the keypad, the garage door opened and there sat the definition of a nondescript car. A beige, eight-year-old Honda sedan. I glanced inside and was very pleased to see it had air conditioning at least.

I threw my gear in the trunk, hopped in, and drove off to cross the border.

Thanks to my complexion, I never had an issue getting into Mexico. I expect my looks didn't slow things down either, other than when a border guard wanted to hit on me.

This was not one of those times and soon I was zipping South on Mexico 2 toward my destination.

Chapter 20 Four – Los Mochis

After a brief rest nap in Hermosillo, I was glad to hit the outskirts of Los Mochis. I was quite hungry and loved Sonoran style Mexican food so decided I would eat before I found the house. I enjoyed some great food and a single margarita and soon was back on my way.

As I turned onto Numero 4 street, I began to scan the houses. I spotted a nice looking two storey that I hoped was mine, but it wasn't. My house, number 1529, was a run-down looking dump directly across the street. There was a carport, closed off with heavy metal gates, and another gate across the door. I reached through the door gate and located a keypad on the backside of the wall where I punched in a code.

The door opened into the caged garage, and I went to an electrical panel where a second keypad was located underneath it. That one got me into the house. It was nothing on the outside and only slightly better inside. At least it looked comfortable and clean so I couldn't whine too much. I located the stash of weapons in the back of a closet behind a false panel and began to do an inventory.

They had everything I had asked for. My favorite close quarters pistols, two 32 calibre Beretta Tomcats.

They were small, easy to conceal and still packed a reasonable punch. There were multiple clips, half loaded with cut-face mushroom slugs and the other half with armor piercing rounds. I had also requested my favorite sniper rifles.

The McMillan TAC 50 is the sniper rifle you hear the most about in long range kills. It is listed with an effective firing range of 1,800 metres. There was recently a Canadian sniper however, using that rifle, who has a confirmed kill shot of a Taliban fighter at 3,540 meters or a little over TWO MILES. At that range it took the bullet almost eight seconds to reach its target. I was hoping to be no more than 1,000 meters away, so I wasn't worried.

The other rifle I had was a 22-250. Although the police sniper units and tactical teams typically use a .308 caliber hunting rifle, I prefer the 22-250. It shoots flat and fast and when you load your own shells you can get excellent performance out of it. It can also be much more easily silenced. I kept getting everything ready as I prepared my recon plan for the coming days.

I knew that El Mayo travelled frequently around Sinaloa and Los Mochis. He made that trip at least twice per week, returning to his oceanside house at Topolobampo.

It was only a 24 kilometre drive down highway 22 from Los Mochis but there were many hills and turns. It would be a good place to shoot from and provided many escape routes.

With the current state of the so called "drug war" in Mexico none of these guys were too worried. Many kept rigid schedules and didn't bother with too many alternate routes. I took the truck out of the garage, fueled it up and got it ready to go. There was also a 650 dual sport motorcycle with which you could easily traverse ANY of the desert areas around here.

I packed all the weapons back where they were, everything cleaned and ready to go, and prepared to leave the next day. I drove out while it was still dark and positioned myself in the low hills, about 500 meters off the highway, roughly halfway from Topolobampo. The good thing about this part of Mexico is that you can simply veer off the road and your tracks are gone within an hour, buried by wind-blown, swirling waves of sand.

I spent two weeks watching and waiting, cataloguing all the vehicles. Thanks to high powered binoculars and a spotting scope I was able to see whatever I wanted. Turned out that he and three henchmen made the trip each Tuesday and Friday. They usually stayed over Friday night, returning to Los Mochis before noon on the Saturday.

That would make it easy, provided everything fell into place. I would have to eliminate Claudia Felix, the assassin, on a Monday night for this plan to work. I began surveillance on Claudia. I knew that she favored the company of women so that would be my angle. I tracked her for a week and noted that she spent three nights at the Aruba Fish & Grill restaurant. That was where I would make my play for her.

Assassins were typically a very wary bunch, but she would have no reason to think anyone would be coming after her. Besides, I figured certain I was her type after seeing her with two different women on those three nights. I did one more week of tracking, alternating between the two spots and spent three evenings at the Aruba. I needed her to have seen me so she might have both a comfort level and hopefully, interest.

The following week I would make my move. I went out on the Friday night to the Aruba and "bumped into" Claudia. I have to say she was a striking woman and even up close, I got the Kardashian reference. I played it as cool as possible and finally we bumped into each other in the ladies' room. I gave her my best smile in hopes she would know I was interested. Every now and then, being a powerful looking woman was helpful.

We chatted briefly and when it was time for me to leave, I smiled as I walked by her table and said I hoped to see her soon. As I drove back to the house, I felt positive that she would show on Monday.

I got up early Sunday and loaded the bike into the back of the truck so I could take it out to the hills. Although nobody had seen me in the vehicle, I didn't want to take a chance. I was also planning to send the truck a different direction and blow it up after I took out El Mayo so I could use the bike to get back to my car. I found the spot I would shoot from and covered up the bike under some brush and trees close by.

I drove leisurely back to town and spent the afternoon and evening ensuring everything else was ready. Weapons, fuel, the Honda all gassed up and plenty of water to drink.

I awoke Monday and went for an early run. It always calmed me down to do eight or ten miles and clear my head. I just hung around, had an afternoon nap, and then showered and got ready to go. My plan was to get Claudia away from the Aruba and then slip her a deadly drug cocktail.

Something simple like a roofie to knock her out and then a hot shot of heroin and meth combined. She was known to be a druggie so that would look innocent enough I felt.

I spotted her watching me as I walked through the door in a shorter than average skirt and tight fitting knit top. I knew I looked good, and she appeared to think so as well. I sat at the bar until she eventually came up and started a conversation. We chatted as we sipped on drinks and then she asked if I was staying for dinner. When I said I was she suggested we keep each other company. She smiled broadly when I said that was a great idea.

This was looking far easier than I had expected. I hoped it remained this easy. As I spoke with her, I found myself not believing she could be an assassin. Then again, I supposed I didn't seem like a stone-cold killer either.

We finished our dinner and she asked if I might like to come to her house for a nightcap. It was risky but if she lived alone, and nobody saw me coming or going, it could work. I smiled and told her I would love a nightcap and I would follow her in my truck. As we drove through the narrow dusty streets, I could tell we were close to the house where I was staying.

She rolled into a driveway, and I parked outside on the street as she went into the garage. I hopped out and followed her through the garage door. I was caught a little off guard when she turned and kissed me.

I had never kissed another woman before, so it was certainly strange, but I think I pulled it off. At least I hoped I had pulled it off. I knew I had to get this done as quickly as possible.

The house looked like a million dollars on the inside which was in stark contrast to the outside. The outside was old and weathered. I suppose in this part of Mexico one did not want to display too much wealth. I eagerly accepted a glass of red wine as we walked through the house. It was quite the place, including high end art and other things. As we entered a smaller room, I noticed it was a gallery of sorts. Tiny, but holding some significant pieces of art.

I was stunned when I looked at the wall directly ahead and, bathed in a gentle glow of soft light, was an original Frida Kahlo. She is known as one of the greatest artists in self portraiture. I admired her Self-Portrait with Thorn Necklace and Hummingbird. I knew it was one of her most famous works, but I thought it was kept in a state gallery. I turned to Claudia and said I had only seen such pieces in museums and art galleries.

She smiled at me and said that she had always loved Frida's work as she felt like a bit of a kindred spirit. An accident taking away her ability to do what she loved (medicine) but giving her a whole new passion. She said she simply HAD to have that piece, so she bought it. That was when I noticed a large wall around the corner, completely covered in paint.

As I got closer, I noticed the plaster and realized it was a fresco, the same medium Michelangelo had used in the Sistine Chapel. I was stunned and a little embarrassed to ask, but I had to know. Was this an original Diego Rivera fresco? She smiled broadly and said the house had been in her family for years and this fresco was the reason for the initial purchase. Yes, it was a Rivera! I was simply amazed as we looked through the rest of the room.

Now I knew there would be cameras, and other security equipment. I would have to go over the house top to bottom to ensure there was no record of me being there. Once I was done, I would have to quickly search and destroy any traces I had been there. I continued my diligence in touching as little as possible and remembering every place where I could not avoid leaving a print. I considered not following through with this part of the plan but only briefly. I had my orders, and I was going to carry them out.

Finally, we were back in the living room and Claudia excused herself to use the powder room. As soon as she was out of reach, I spiked her glass with the roofie and awaited her return. It was a faster acting version of the drug and within thirty minutes she was almost comatose on the sofa. I put on my gloves, got the needle out of my purse, and pressed her hand around it, thumb on the plunger. I located a healthy vein in her arm and slowly pressed down on the top of her thumb.

Twenty seconds later she was dead. I left the needle in her arm and positioned her hands appropriately. Then I began to scour the house. I started by getting rid of any evidence there had been two people. I went room to room and finally located recording equipment, along with multiple computer screens behind a well-hidden bookcase door.

I erased the last two hours, reset the clock/timer, and noted the camera locations covering the outside and inside. My truck was out of view of the driveway camera, and I could see an escape path out the back. Thankfully the system was designed to capture photos and videos of everything going on inside the house, but very little of the outside. I felt comfortable I could get away clean.

I slipped out the back and moved quickly down the alley, hoping I could get to the street soon. Thankfully there was a pathway only a few houses up. I jumped in my truck and headed back to my house, glad that part was over.

I parked, got inside, and grabbed a nice hot shower before getting everything double-checked once more for tomorrow.

Chapter 20 Five - Mission Accomplished

I awoke to the vibrating of my alarm and popped out of the bed. I got myself ready to go and packed everything up and moved it into the Honda, in case I was in a hurry when I returned. I hoped I wouldn't be but always better to plan every detail and not need them than the reverse.

It was still very dark as I headed down highway 22, hoping they would leave earlier than usual. I didn't want to sit out in the desert all day waiting.

I got to my spot and uncovered the bike and got it ready, using the lights of the truck to guide me. Once I was ready, I prepared the truck with the charges needed, and pointed it away from the direction I would leave on the bike. Draped with camo netting it would be impossible to see from that distance.

I moved closer to the roadway and prepared my rifle. I had decided to go with the 22-250 due to the silencer. I knew I could be accurate with it from 1,000 metres if needed but I was positioned, under camouflage, only about two hundred metres from the road. I then began to scan the road with my binoculars, looking closely at each vehicle as it approached. Thankfully there were very few that travelled this road.

Finally, I saw the black escalade that I now knew belonged to Zambada. It had very distinctive rims as well as a small dent at the back of the driver side passenger door. I was very happy to see they were alone, no other vehicles with them. I checked ahead and behind them and saw no other vehicles for miles in either direction. A real stroke of luck, for me at least.

I sighted in the drivers' side front tire and slowly squeezed the trigger sending the slug on its way. If there was a crash and they died in a fire that would be good too, but a bullet in El Mayo's head would be more likely to trigger the desired war between the cartels. Through my scope, I watched the tire explode and the vehicle veer off the road on my side of the highway.

It crashed front first into a sand dune, and I waited for people to emerge. Two men staggered out of the rear of the vehicle and when I saw neither was El Mayo I got concerned. I watched as the driver got out and then was relieved when Zambada got out of the passenger side. I sighted in on his head as he moved slowly around the vehicle. When he was clear and leaning on the SUV, I eased the trigger towards me until I felt the discharge.

I watched his head explode as the modified slug blew apart into pieces inside his skull. He slumped to the ground and was certainly dead, no doubt a gaping hole where the back of his skull used to be.

I quickly acquired the other two and took them out as well, leaving the driver. There needed to be someone to tell the story and spread the word. I shot him once in the leg to slow him down. Even if he had a phone I would still be long gone before help arrived.

I packed everything up, buried the rifle in a hole I had dug previously and prepared the truck. I had wired the steering wheel and aimed the truck where it should be able to travel at least two miles.

I got everything ready, started it up and set the bomb timer for ten minutes. I made sure the bike started and ran and then sent the truck off on its short journey.

I rode quickly in the other direction, staying in the dunes out of view of the highway for a good five miles. Just before I turned toward the highway I stopped and watched a large cloud of black smoke as the truck exploded. It was less than ten minutes more and I had the bike stowed in the garage and was gathering the rest of my things. Even though this was a safe house of sorts, I ensured that I sanitized everything. There were multiple containers of bleach and even lye in the house so one could get rid of all evidence.

I closed everything up and got into the little Honda to make my escape.

I had decided I would return via the Nogales crossing as it would support my whole photographer cover. I also wanted to visit the La Roca restaurant on my way. They served outstanding food and there were also a bunch of souvenir places there. Another great way to support a tourist cover.

I went back up highway 15 and then took the exit to Nogales. Thankfully, an uneventful drive. I had a couple of roadside naps in small towns and planned to hit La Roca for dinner. I managed to stay awake and rolled in about 5:30 and I was hungry. I would eat a great meal and then head towards the border, planning to stay overnight in Tucson.

The food was outstanding. I could eat their avocado salads every day! I relaxed and rested my mind as I took in the sights after dinner.

I walked amongst the many boutiques in this area. I knew that arriving at the border between 8:00 and 9:00 PM would be ideal as many Arizonans make the quick trip here for the restaurants and shops, returning around that time. The walking gate is also very close if that was needed.

I rolled up to the border, greeted by a gruff looking agent. I suppose my Hispanic looks may have piqued his interest. He asked more than a couple of questions after taking my passport and license but then waved me through. It was good to be back on US soil and I went directly into Tucson to find a nice hotel.

I felt like soaking in a long hot bath with a bottle of wine and that is exactly what I did. Enjoying a tasty bottle of Malbec was always a great way for me to relax.

The next day I drove over to California and returned to my apartment. Cartel activity was already showing on the local news with the assassination of El Mayo leading the headlines. It looked like things would play out just as whomever issued the orders wanted. Even though I had just killed four people I had a sense of accomplishment and calmness.

I went back to my usual routine and hit the gym hard, running into Hector my first day back. We had a good chat and I told him I had gone to visit a friend down in Mexico. I saw no danger in letting him know where I was. I knew that I could not be connected to anything that had happened down there. As we trained, I wondered what my next assignment would be and when Cato would get in touch.

Chapter 20 Six – Reenlist??

I was contacted the next day by someone claiming to work with Vice Admiral Bourque. I was told where and when I was to be at a specific location and to arrive with an open mind. I wondered what the heck this was about and tried multiple times to contact Cato, with no luck. I was contacted via a secure channel, so it had to be legitimate, but it still seemed odd.

I arrived and was directed to a bench in the park. There was a man sitting there and as I got closer, I confirmed it was Bourque. He didn't stand or shake my hand or anything. He simply said hello. As I sat, he looked at me and said he heard I had done some good work. He went on to explain that he really did think it was time for a female navy SEAL. He had my attention to be sure.

I listened intently as he explained it would not be easy and, to eliminate any suspicion, I would need to complete SQT again. I was a little choked when he said that, but I knew immediately I wanted, maybe even needed, to be the first female navy SEAL. I looked at him and said whatever it takes, I will do it. He stood and said I would be contacted soon, make sure I stayed in town.

That is exactly what I did. The following week a few packages showed up with all my required navy gear and uniforms along with a reporting slip for SQT. The next class was starting in four weeks.

I trained like a madman for the whole time, taking only the last two days off. I reported to the facility and quickly got back into everything as if I had never left. My story was that after initial training I had a medical situation. It had to be dealt with and that was why nobody there recognized me from the previous training.

I suppose I could have whined about it, but I took it as a challenge to try to best what I did previously. To make a long story short, I made it through everything and was soon standing in a line with my fellow graduates about to receive my second pin and knife.

It was great to leave SQT with actual teammates and finally feel the full force of achievement and pride in what I had done. Everyone there seemed to be on my side, but I would soon discover that wasn't really the case. I accepted my trident and then moved over to the knife ceremony.

I was shocked to see the same name, Stephen Mills, on my knife. I was more surprised when I discovered they had given me back my OWN knife from my previous ceremony.

All the ceremonies complete and a small party and, as I had previously done, I was dispatched to the island for additional training.

Everything was about the same on the island. Similar challenges, some of the same leaders but it felt different somehow. People seemed to be putting a little more into the fights and battles. I could not determine if it was in my head or if they really WERE trying harder. I chalked it up to them wanting to challenge me, especially the couple who knew I had already been there.

In what seemed like no time I was done, having already formed what would be lifelong friendships with a couple of the guys. Now it was a matter of where I was going and with whom.

There was still additional tactical training but that would come once assigned to a team.

Chapter 20 Seven – Foxtrot

Within two weeks I was advised that I would be part of SEAL Team 7. So here I was, an actual Navy SEAL. NOW I could tell my parents I hoped. I received my orders and reported to a different camp, meeting up with a group of others. Most didn't realize at first that I was one of them.

We all gathered in a central mess and started to get acquainted. Many seemed to assume I was an intelligence officer or something non-combat related. As I was shaking the hand of one of the guys, I heard a booming voice from across the room. It was Boone, yelling out that he should watch himself or that "chick" will kick his ass. He came over and we slapped hands and hugged with a big pat on the back.

I met Boone at SQT and was immediately in his corner. He seemed the most like one of my brothers. He treated me as an equal right out of the gate and was soon telling anyone who would listen that he wouldn't be my sparring partner because it hurt too much! The mood of some of those around me seemed to change. I'm sure they thought they showed nothing, but I could tell. I had a real knack for reading people, something that would keep me in good stead throughout my career.

No worries for me though. I was confident that during the rigorous training exercises we would go through I would prove to be more than capable. Boone and me both had the same rank, E-6, or Petty Officer

First Class. The SEALS used standard Navy ranks, just as every other service special division used the ranks of their own branch.

As a nod to our completion of BUD/S and SQT successful SEALS skipped a couple ranks and were set at E-6, also noted as PO1. It wasn't a large difference in rank, but it was two steps up from the bottom with the associated slight increase in pay.

SEAL teams fall under the purview of Naval Special Warfare Groups, 1 or 2. 1 for West and 2 for East. Each SEAL team consists of six platoons. These platoons are commonly called teams as well and are comprised of two officers and 13 enlisted men. I wonder if I would be considered just one of the thirteen or not? Each platoon was structured the same consisting of a platoon Chief, Master Chief Petty Officer, and his XO, typically an E-6 or Leading CPO. The enlisted men below that each gravitated toward specific duties.

As I surveyed the room, wondering if this was my platoon or not, I was reminded when I noticed the designation that this was SEAL Team 7. Soon a gruff looking guy stood at the front of the room and announced that he was the Officer in Charge.

He was basically the leader in the office of the operational team. He went on to explain that this was the Foxtrot platoon. He said some of us may be aware that the leadership of this team had been relieved of their duty only four weeks previous.

He gravely stated there were team issues that would not be discussed. He wanted us to know that ANY transgressions or situations that brought Foxtrot into the light, specifically bad light, would result in immediate dishonorable discharge. He finished up and introduced our ground leader, the top man in the field, Master Chief Kennedy, henceforth known as Foxtrot 1. We all now listened very closely, a singular focus on our leader. He explained that this platoon was a mix of new and old. The best men from Foxtrot were retained and there were six newly minted SEALS added. Our lives now depended on one another, and we would rise to the top as a team.

He looked out into the group and said Fox 2 is that rather large fellow in the centre of the group. He was the second-in-charge. I looked him up and down and realized he could better be described as tall rather than large. He looked like an in-shape NBA player, small power forward size. He appeared to be about six-five and I was sure solid muscle. You were not in any SEAL platoon without being a star in all categories and it was plain to see he was.

In a nod to the Lakers of old he was nicknamed Magic. Good old Earvin Johnson, one of the best guards to ever play the game. He even resembled him ever so slightly, at least when he smiled. We were told to grab some beers, relax, and get to know one another. I went straight over to Boone to try and have a quick chat about the whole SEAL team 7 business but was cut off by Master Chief Kennedy. He said he needed a word with me.

We walked outside for privacy, and he said he was glad to have me on the team and was looking forward to seeing what I could do. He smiled and said that we both knew that I was the first female to ever make it to a platoon and there were a few things to consider. He asked if I had any nicknames I could use as we would need to work to keep this quiet. A minimal number of people had been read in on my selection and it would be best if it stayed that way for now. I told him that when I played ball, I had picked up the nickname Sunny. I said it was a nod to my positive outlook. He smiled and said Sunny would work fine.

As if on cue, Foxtrot 2 stepped out the door and shook my hand. Welcome to Foxtrot platoon he said. We are going to rebuild this unit and soon be known as the best. For now, let's get back inside and get everyone acquainted.

We spent the rest of the evening doing more talking than drinking. It was clear nobody had any intention of getting intoxicated, even the original Foxtrot operators. As we closed up for the night, we were advised to be at the obstacle course at 7:00 AM in full gear.

We were then shown to the warehouse where each of us had a large gear cage. Each was labelled with a number. I was glad I'm not a superstitious type when I was told my number was 13.

Chapter 20 Eight – Train, Train, Train

Everyone was gearing up at their lockers at oh-six-hundred, as nobody wanted to be late. We readied ourselves and walked as a group to the obstacle course. We arrived at 6:45, not at all surprised to find Master Chief Kennedy and Fox 2 already there.

We stood around a large table and listened as Fox 1 told us that training was key to operational readiness. We needed to be 100% invested in taking care of our teammates and completing our missions. All our lives would depend on an unwavering commitment to this concept. Hooyah, the group yelled in unison. As such we would begin some obstacle course training and then head to the gun range. In almost one voice, we yelled out another Hooyah as we moved to the start.

Each branch of the services has their own version of this acknowledgement or call of support. The Air Force has HUA, which stands for Heard, Understood and Acknowledged. The Marines and Seabee's have Hoorah and the army has Hooah. They all basically serve the same purpose.

The Hooyah, used by SEALs, is said to have originated with the Underwater Demolition Teams (UDT`s) in World War 2. It was heard thousands of times during training.

Magic was waiting at the start line. He explained the course was different and more treacherous than any we had seen. We had to keep aware of all surroundings at all times.

There may also be simulated attacks while running the course, so we needed to move quickly but always remain vigilant. As there were thirteen of us, Magic said he would join a group to make the numbers even. He took the six standing to his left, which included me, and said you're with me, let's go. He turned to the other group and advised them to wait ten minutes and then get on course. He added that if we did get attacked there were to be no weapons of any sort used. All defense or attack would be purely hand to hand.

We started on course setup with Magic at lead, Boone covering the rear and the rest of us in the middle. Two covering each side while the fifth was watching Fox 2. We began to move quickly. No more than a minute into the obstacles we were suddenly being drenched from above with fire hoses simulating a driving rain. No shock there, and we all kept moving like nothing happened. Water to a SEAL is like air to everyone else.

We stopped at a corner of thick trees as Fox 2 directed the two on each side to branch out and then move slowly ahead. The rest of the group remained.

We had a commentary on our coms earpieces from Fox 2 telling us about enemy camps etc. Just then three attackers came out of the dense brush toward us. We were far enough away from the group we knew we would be on our own for at least sixty seconds, if not longer.

I wasn't too surprised when two of the three came at me. I figured there would be many tests like this, and I fully expected to have to prove myself more capable than the men. I wasn`t too worried because I was already relatively certain I WAS more capable than many of them. We still had our full gear on, and they were not encumbered by anything other than small packs. I quickly spotted an area with two trees that I could use to my advantage.

I didn`t want to hurt anyone as this was training, but they told us it was REAL training and we needed to view it as life or death. I placed the trees between the two attackers and myself as Rusty (yes, he was a redhead) yelled our location into the coms.

As the attackers rounded the trees, I went at the first one to emerge hitting him hard in the midsection with a kick. I knew he was winded and wouldn't just pop up. The second one came at me, and I slipped his grip, spun around, and locked in a choke hold.

As the other stood up, I told him to back off or his buddy was dead. They both raised their hands in the air as I spotted Rusty escorting his attacker my way.

When he got to me Magic and two others came out of the trees. He just smiled and said all good, let`s get back on track. The rest of the morning went similarly. Various attempts were made to break up the group, but nothing worked, and we all emerged relatively unscathed at the finish. We waited for the other group to finish before heading over for chow.

We chatted over lunch about strategy in various situations and then went to the range. We stood in front of tables loaded with all kinds of sidearms and rifles. I spotted the rifle of choice for SEALs and went to it. The M4A1 was a superior weapon. You could equip it to do many things thanks to all the modifications and accessories done within the SOPMOD program.

SOPMOD is the Special Operations Peculiar Modification program which worked with the base rifle to customize it for special ops. There were handles, laser sights, sound suppressors and even a grenade launcher attachment. This weapon gave you the greatest flexibility and if one malfunctioned or was lost, you could quickly change to another type to fulfill that purpose. It reminded me of a toy gun I had when I was a child with all the attachments. It just lacked batteries and lights!

We were told to each grab a Sig Sauer P226R nine mm pistol and an HK .45 ACP. Two very different pistols, each good in its own right. I still preferred my Berettas but knew that I wouldn't be allowed to use them here. I would be a laughingstock if anyone found out I preferred a .32 calibre "pea shooter".

Everyone was very well trained and knowledgeable on all current weapons, so we grabbed ammo, clips and the pistols and got in position. We were taken through numerous exercises including single hand, quick draw, and standard stance. As one might expect, everyone scored well at multiple distances. We were told to select one pistol and then go to the situation range. That is an automated series of rooms where different threats and non-threats pop out at you. You had to quickly determine danger or not and decide to fire or not fire in a split second.

After a couple of hours, and multiple runs, we were told to return to the armory. The range instructors had been informed by our team leaders the strengths of the various members. Rusty and I were chosen from the group and taken to a different area. We arrived and saw that it was a medium and long-range target field. In front of us was a selection of rifles including the M4A1, which wasn't even applicable here. It was more of a short-range assault rifle rather than a sniper tool.

There was a series of sniper rifles too, all equipped with some sort of suppressor. I was told to take the fifty cal and set up on the side. Even with a muzzle brake and a suppressor that weapon packed quite a punch, but its range was unequalled. This was one on one training. My instructor said that on the teams we would frequently be shooting alone, no spotter to gauge wind, distance, or any other factors which could affect the shot.

I laid on the ground after preparing the rifle and began to spot various targets down range. The built-in range finder in the sight had a plus minus of about 10 yards so that would be plenty for me. My instructor told me to search for the black SUV and evaluate the targets before taking a shot. I identified mine, noting it was about 1,300 yards distant. In my mind I calculated for wind and curvature, as minimal as it was, and slowly squeezed the trigger. I remained calm in place as I watched the head of the target blown into nothingness.

This went on for the rest of the day with Rusty and me changing positions and weapons multiple times. There was a hill behind us that we had to run up and down before the rest of the firing practice. You had to get back to the top, settle quickly, calm your breathing, and then execute the shot.

I think we both did well.

This training, with various targets and weapons, would become our regular routine when on base. We would either be doing general training, or the range would be setup for a specific mission.

Either way the training and honing of our skills never stopped. That was the recipe to a long life when being an operator.

Chapter 20 Nine – My First Mission as a SEAL

Finally, the time had arrived. The new team members were briefed separately by Fox 1. He and Magic explained that this mission for us was solely about watching and learning. We would stay close to the overwatch team and be equipped with the same coms so we could simulate being on the ground. It wasn't what I expected but I realized that trial by fire really wasn't an option in this case. No matter how much you trained, live fire was always a fluid situation.

We joined the rest of our team and were told we were being spun up the next morning at oh five hundred. 5:00 AM comes quickly but it's not like we hadn't spent the last two years of our lives being ready to go any time, any where. I slept quite well considering but awoke somewhat anxious. We were all at our cages joking and telling stories at 4:00 AM. Quite a few jabs and comments from the original team directed at us newbies but nothing gender-specific or directly at me. Just the usual banter and pseudo-hazing.

That was until the topic of conversation came around to sniper work. They were relentless bugging me about makeup smudging my scope and how could I shoot like that. It was all good-natured ribbing though and it felt good to know that I was part of the team. If they would have left me completely alone that would have concerned me.

I shot back as much as I took and that seemed to gain me some street cred with the boys. I was never happier that I had four older brothers to teach me!

Finally, we were ready, and we walked as a group out to the tarmac.

The Navy SEAL teams don't have their own aircraft. They are typically transported by other branches of the military. Most frequently the SEALs are flown to destination by SOAR, the Army's Special Operations Aviation Regiment. Longer distance missions are often made aboard the massive C-17 cargo aircraft. These can carry a full platoon with support, overwatch and targeting experts. Once on target, operators are often delivered using the highly modified MH 60 black hawk helo, called the Quiet One due to its stealth capability.

Depending on the mission, SEALs may deploy by helo and ropes, high altitude low opening parachute drops, or simply land vehicles. They are also backed up and monitored by a series of drones, the use of which began with the SEAL teams. Drones are becoming more and more prevalent in the US military. They allow for a calmness and focus because the pilots have no worry about being shot down or killed in action. From the 4.2-pound Raven to the 13-pound Puma these UAVs (Unmanned Aerial Vehicles) can be easily transported anywhere.

In addition to these drones, which are primarily used for monitoring, locating, and painting targets, there is the Reaper. The MQ-9 Reaper is a deadly weapon. It carries the Hellfire missiles, laser-guided bombs, and other classified firepower. They can also fly much higher than regular aircraft making them much more difficult to detect and defend against.

The overwatch team used satellites and drones to gain a picture of the teams and their target(s). They kept us posted in real-time with all that intel.

Before takeoff we gathered around a storage box in the rear of the aircraft. The sides were lined with seats and there was also a row of hammock style bunks. The newbies watched intently as the guys were told about their target, location, and other data. We were headed to Islamabad in Pakistan where we were going to neutralize a terrorist cell and training area. It had to be accomplished by boots on the ground so it would look like tribal infighting and not a US strike.

The US no longer has any air bases in Pakistan so entry would be at night via HALO drop. That was the High Altitude, Low Opening parachute jumping that we had all trained for extensively. As we got closer to Pakistani air space everyone checked and rechecked their gear. We stayed close to the computer screens as our overwatch team began searching and targeting. Once confirmed, the GPS coordinates would be transmitted to the ground team.

The cargo door opened and one after another, our teammates jumped into the darkness. In no time the screens showed the heat signatures of our team along with the location they were headed to. Each team member wore a helmet camera as well as an invisible beacon on the top of their helmets. From here we could see each of our guys and, in the distance, the heat signatures of multiple targets.

At a glance, they seemed to be outnumbered two or three to one. Knowing what I now knew, I felt those were pretty good odds...for us! It felt like our operators could go to war with NO weapons and still emerge victorious.

In what seemed like no time, it was over. I alternated viewing the targeting screen and the helmet cam video to catch as much of the action as I could. I was fascinated seeing the surgical precision of the operation. As the plane banked, I watched the team moving en masse toward what I assumed was an exfil point. They would be extracted by a Black Hawk helo and then delivered to the nearest US air location in Afghanistan, where we had just landed.

Bagram Air Base was one of six USA bases in Afghanistan. The team would be brought back here. As we waited for our comrades to arrive, we sat around discussing various details of the strike.

What we all really wanted though was to speak directly with our team, hear what they had to say. Soon the helos landed and there were high fives all around as the team headed to the briefing room. We were told to stay outside for this one which did not impress any of us.

We wanted to be in on the action, ALL the action. That time would come sooner than expected. Finally, the boys strutted out of the room, and we went outside to sit around and have a cold beer or two. We knew we could not get drunk or anything as we were still in a dangerous place. There was also the possibility of a second mission related to this one. We all talked, told stories, and joked about anything and everything. That seemed to be how most of us destressed.

That was when I discovered that one of the operators had been in the Canadian National Police Force, the RCMP. He had dual citizenship so when he found the RCMP not totally to his liking he wanted to be a SEAL.

The Royal Canadian Mounted Police were known the world over, and Dan would tell you anything you wanted to know about being a Mountie. When the guys found out about his background one of them did some searching and decided on his nickname.

Everyone was soon calling the poor guy, Dudley. Apparently, Dudley Do-Right was a character on a TV show in Canada.

Unlike the typical RCMP member, Dudley was a dim witted but cheerful Mountie. I would later find some references on you tube and felt kind of bad for Dan, I mean Dudley. Oh well, that was the way it worked around here. Everyone was known and bugged about something. That was one way you knew that you belonged, people felt comfortable giving you the gears.

We all hit the rack early, after we had prepared and rechecked all our weapons and packs along with new chutes. Preparedness was key to survival here. We were all at the mess eating around 7:00 AM when our team leader came in and called us to the ready room.

Chapter Thirty – The Real Deal

Once we were all in the room, we were told there was another HVT (High Value Target) we needed to address. We were told that it would require the complete team. I had no butterflies or nerves when hearing this for the first time. I had been trained extensively and, unknown to these guys, had already been close to here, on the ground. I wanted so badly to share with them who I had eliminated but I knew I could not.

We all listened closely to the plan. The targets, potential locations, access and more. It would, as usual, be a night operation and we would be dropped via helo in the mountain range closest to the border with Pakistan. We would navigate across, with all our gear, and emerge from the hills ready to annihilate a terrorist training camp.

On the good side, ALL people at this location were targets. There were NO innocents, no non-combatants. It would have been easier to simply blow it sky-high with drones but there was another concern.

There was one person who needed to be taken alive, which would be a challenge. As a top man in the Taliban, our government wanted the intelligence he could provide.

Violence was escalating and control of various regions was in a state of flux. Although there have been efforts made to legitimize the Taliban politically, they continue to resist that option. As recently as October of last year 10 election candidates were assassinated by the Taliban. A message needed to be sent.

The Kunar region is currently under Taliban control. It is a strategic target due to its proximity to the border with Pakistan. The Taliban has a history of moving in and out of the area, using Pakistan to both hide and stage fighters and equipment. The commander in the Kunar area is Ahmadshah. He is an influential leader, and it was believed he, and his electronic devices, would carry a great deal of information about the Taliban in the rest of country. We needed to gain control of him and the area before any of those electronics could be destroyed or erased.

We spent the balance of the day preparing and mapping out points of attack as well as defining our exfil point. The target was in a valley in the Kunar province with mountains on each side that paralleled the Pakistani border. The terrain was rough but navigable. We reviewed satellite maps in detail and pinned numerous GPS coordinates to guide us. Once we were done, we ate together and then hit our racks for some sleep prior to leaving.

At 23:00 hours were all on a helo and headed toward our destination. We had to risk flying quite low to avoid radar which exposed us to possible ground fire. I recalled my mission to take out the guy that destroyed Extortion 17 and a slight smile came to my face. One of the guys asked what I was happy about. I smiled more broadly and said killing bad guys makes me happy. He just nodded in agreement.

In no time we had all dropped and were gathering on the ground burying chutes and lines. They were nondescript chutes with no markings and had been sourced within Afghanistan so would not be out of place even if they were found. We had no patches or other identification on rucks or anything else either.

The trek was close to four miles, but we did it quickly. About 1,000 yards out, Boone and I stayed behind on high ground, each of us equipped with .50 calibre rifles with all the goodies. We spread out, as the rest of the team continued, and took up complimentary positions that would allow us to cover almost the whole compound.

The coms in our ears came to life as our overwatch began to detail the numbers of people and locations. It was easy to tell who the sentries were, so they would be the first taken out. Once the team gained access to the building, we would work in concert with overwatch to get our man out.

As we saw our team approach from two sides, Boone and I took out six sentries posted outside. We then trained our sights on the building itself, watching and listening. We would later find out that it went rather quickly. They were completely unprepared for this attack and, even though our team was outnumbered, the enemy was no match.

The team moved as one, clearing room by room. Bad guys jumping out to shoot only to be felled, many times before even getting off one shot. Then we heard that all were dead, and they had Ahmadshah in their possession.

Boone and I had to move quickly as the helo would be at the exfil point soon and the team would likely arrive before us, even dragging a hostage. We gathered everything up, including spent brass and moved through the hills with purpose and determination. We arrived at almost the same time as the rest of the team to a round of high fives. The helos got us out of there quietly and back to the base safely.

The Afghani Special Forces (NDS) would claim the victory as far as the public was aware. The NDS even claimed to have assassinated Ahmadshah, but that was a blatant lie. He was in our possession and already being interrogated. It was happening right on the base in a secure sea can and one can only imagine what was going on in there.

We had also secured a lot of electronics that would add a great deal to our intel about the Taliban throughout Afghanistan. Overall, the mission was a huge win and the debrief was very positive.

Once in the air, it all seemed a distant memory as we hitched a ride back to Naval Amphibious Base Coronado in California. Coronado sits across the bay from San Diego and was created when the bay was dredged to allow passage of large Navy ships in WW2. NAB Coronado is slightly over 1,000 acres in size and provides more than 7,500 yards of beaches. There are 30 different commands stationed here and over 5,000 personnel. Thanks to the water, beaches, and varied terrain, it is the ideal training ground for many of the Navy forces, especially the SEALs.

It was great to get back there and get reacclimated. I really enjoyed that area as there was always lots to do and, of course, a great naval presence. It made relaxing quite easy to accomplish. During our last meeting before liberty, we were advised that we had been selected to test some new equipment. That was certainly not great news. I didn't want to be a guinea pig, I wanted to fight!

Oh well, one of the main tenets of being in any branch of our military is that you do what you are told and commit 100%. Still, I knew I would be glad to get home to my humble apartment for a break.

Chapter Thirty 1 – My Aunt

Before I could get off base, I was told the Master Chief wanted to meet with me. It wasn't terribly out of the ordinary for the team leader to want to speak with individuals one on one, but I was still concerned. I went into his office and after being asked to sit down he told me had been contacted by a lawyer. He was very sad to tell me that my aunt had passed away. He went on to explain that I could have up to a week of bereavement leave but that if I needed more, we might be able to figure something out.

Early the next morning I was on a plane to Portland with a rental car booked to get me to the lawyer's office. I was in a fog the whole flight, memories of my aunt flooding my head. The lawyer had been a family friend for years and I was glad for that. He would truly understand the loss I was experiencing.

My aunt didn't live right in Portland but in a quaint seaside town just south of there called Old Orchard Beach. It was a short but beautiful drive down the coast, and I couldn't help but go directly to the beach first. I had so loved walking through the town and out onto the pier.

Thankfully it was a warm and sunny day, so I parked and began to stroll. Everything was so familiar to me. From my favorite little candy shop to the ice cream parlour, it was a familiarity that brought me comfort at a sad time.

It had all the typical seaside architecture and colors one would expect. Soft hues of blues, greens and yellows were everywhere. Memory after memory came back and I soon found myself smiling.

My aunt was such a wonderful woman, the determined, artistic contrast to my mother but very clearly her sister. Her and my mom were estranged for reasons unknown to me, and it was doubtful my mother would even show. I had long ago accepted the situation and knew there was nothing I could do to change it. I simply stopped letting it bother me. I returned to my car and drove to the lawyer's office.

A shingle hung above the street-side entrance to what looked more like a beach house than an office. As I entered the door a rumpled, grey-haired fellow came up and hugged me, telling me he was so sorry for our loss. I had not seen him in forever and likely wouldn't have recognized him on the street but soon we were chatting like old friends.

He explained my aunt had already made her own funeral arrangements but added he did need to talk to me about the will. He led me back to a plain, but nicely appointed office that looked more like a sea captain's den than anything else.

He pointed me to a couple of chairs with a small table between them. I felt so comfortable in the large, cushy leather armchair positioned to provide a perfect ocean view.

Turned out that my aunt had investments and, rather than give me a sum of money, she had him create a Life Income Fund for me. I was a bit shocked when he told me that I would be receiving a little more than $2,000 per month for the rest of my life.

Risking my life as a SEAL I currently made only $3,249.00 per month!

He also said that she had left me the house in California as she knew that was where I always wanted to live. I really liked that house and made it a point to visit her there whenever we were in California at the same time.

I got all the details required, found out about the service, and left. I went directly back to the pier recalling the times we had spent there. Enjoying the games and even a ride or two. The lawyer had said the service would be a simple one and that her wish was to be cremated. She wanted half her ashes spread here, in her beloved Atlantic Ocean and the other half in California. He told me he would give me two urns the day after the service for this purpose.

As I walked aimlessly up and down the pier, I decided I should stop into the restaurant where we always used to eat. It was a perfect sunny day, exactly the type of day that we would spend time together. I looked down at the old, weathered timbers that made up the pier, marvelling that it was still solid. Rough hewn planks nailed down with large, rusty spikes set on top of an intricate, weaving foundation of wood extending down to the ocean floor.

I wandered into the restaurant and stared out at the water from the top deck as I ate and had a Mai tai, my aunt's favorite drink. They were too sweet for me, but this was all about her and I knew she would appreciate me having one.

I slept like a log that evening. Perhaps the cool salt breeze and just being there relaxed me? I awoke refreshed but immediately a little down as I recalled why I was there. I dressed and went to the service. There were quite a few people as my aunt seemed to know everybody, everywhere. She was a real people magnet thanks to her always sunny disposition and positive outlook. It was nice to see but I was glad when it was over. I was tired of shaking hands, being hugged, and accepting condolences. I just wanted to be alone with my thoughts and memories now.

I didn't sleep much that night as I knew what the next day would bring.

I took my time in the morning, warming my hands on the steaming cup of coffee as I waited. Finally, I went to the lawyer's office to collect the two urns. They were in the shape of books, something I had never seen. I was glad they were not traditional looking urns. That really wasn't my aunt's thing. I took them both, thanked him and shook his hand as I returned to my car.

He had arranged for a small boat to take me out and motor parallel to the shore. When we were in front of the portion of the beach where we spent the most time, I opened the book and slowly let the ashes fall into the sea. I was sad but glad that she entrusted this with me and that I would be her final contact with this earth. As much as I had valued being here, while regretting the reasons why, I couldn't get out of there fast enough.

THE FIRST FEMALE NAVY SEAL

I had an early flight out of the Portland Jetport and was anxious to go. I returned to my hotel, leaving the windows wide open so I could sleep to the sounds of the waves washing gently up onto the beach. I never tired of that sound and looking out at the ocean.

It seemed like the whole time had passed in a blur as I sat on the plane. I put on my headphones, selected my favorite playlist, and closed my eyes. I slept for quite a long while and awoke with only two hours remaining in the flight. I began to think about where to spread the balance of her ashes. They were safely in the overhead compartment in my backpack.

With all the lost luggage these days there was no way I was letting her out of my sight.

The plane landed smoothly, and I reached up to grab my pack and get going. The crowds shuffled out of the jetway like cattle in a chute and soon headed different directions. I located my car quickly and exited the parkade onto the freeway. Every now and then my mind would drift, and I would veer out of the lane slightly, quickly jarred back to reality by the sound of my tires hitting the cat's eyes in the pavement.

Still in a bit of a daze I rolled up to her, I suppose mine now, house. It was close to the beach, not far from Newport, and a really great place. I couldn't believe she had left this to me. It was a beautiful home and had so many memories for me. I turned the key in the lock and swung open the heavy, iron framed wooden door.

I am not a crier but as the door closed behind me, I was overcome with sadness. I knew my aunt was in a good place and she had lived a wonderful life, it was me for whom I felt bad. She had always been a positive influence on me. Sometimes, when my parents would be really driving me, I would talk with her in secret. She was always supportive and encouraged me to do great things.

I just wandered around the house for a few hours, reminding myself of all our good times. I didn't think I could sleep there that evening, so I put her ashes up on the mantle, locked everything up again and went home.

I wasn't sure I would even move in full time at this point. Time would tell.

It took me about a week to plan where and when I would distribute her ashes. I think I always knew where I would go. Although she lived close to Newport, we always enjoyed going to Huntington Beach. We would often eat lunch there while she was in California. Whether it was at Duke's right on the beach, Ruby's at the end of the pier or the patio at Fred's, we always ate well and enjoyed our times together.

I had my plan. I would take my book-shaped urn with me and start with a stroll along the beach. I would then have lunch at Duke's at a table right against the walkway and the sand. I could look out at the Huntington Beach pier and Ruby's and pretend she was still sitting right across from me. I had a friend with a boat who would take me out after lunch so I could complete her journey for her.

When the day arrived, I felt a sense of calmness. Neither happy nor sad I was ready. Ready to fulfil my aunt's wishes and truly say goodbye.

As I walked along the beach, at the water's edge, I took in all the sights. I smiled when I saw the Huntington Beach lifeguard tower. The late morning sun lighting it up like a beacon. That was where they filmed the TV show Baywatch.

I can tell you, the real-life lifeguards there put the TV ones to shame. My aunt used to comment on a lot of those men when we walked past. I smiled when one cut across in front of me, smiled and said hello. I admired him, not in a girl-boy way but, as an athlete.

He was head to toe sinewy muscle and reminded me a little of my father. Now, THERE was an athlete and physical specimen. I know a lot of who I am came from my Dad. People even said that I resembled him more than my mom, but I think a lot of that was because I looked Hispanic like he is.

I arrived at Duke's and ordered a Mai Tai. I felt I really had to. As I sat there enjoying the tastiest fish tacos ever, I smiled as I noticed all the spots where we spent time together. Whether we were on the path, the boardwalk, or the pier, we were non-stop chatting about everything and anything when we were together. I had such great memories of her and all these spots.

I finished up my food and drink and drove over to the nearby marina just North of the City of Huntington Beach. Soon we were out skimming the waves as we motored back and forth a couple of miles from shore. After a bit my buddy slowed the boat and asked if I was ready. I smiled and told him that my aunt wouldn't want a slow speed drop.

I told him to open up the throttles and get us moving. Soon we were skimming the tops of the waves as I opened the book and let the wind draw her ashes from inside. It looked like a trail of smoke, and I smiled as I watched until there were no more ashes. I closed the book urn back up and returned it to my backpack. We cruised back to his slip, and I took off almost right away. I wasn't really wanting to talk to anyone about anything.

Soon I was back in my own apartment and then wondering what was next for me? Where would my team be sent?

In two days, I was back in Coronado warmly welcomed by everyone. That evening a few of us, including Boone, headed out to a waterfront bar in old town. They asked me questions and as I shared more and stories, they were all saying they wished they could have met her. We didn't stay out too late, but I was happy they were there for me. They truly felt like family now.

The next morning in the ready room we were told there was a hostage situation and we had been selected. We would be spun up early to get close to the area where we were needed.

Chapter Thirty 2 – Somalia

Once we were all seated in the ready room, we were told that Somali pirates had taken over an oil tanker. They had captured the crew comprised of sixteen Sri-Lankans and ten Americans. They had made multiple demands including ransom for the people and a threat to blow up the tanker and release its cargo of more than 1.4 million barrels of oil.

The ship was in a very sensitive fishing area and that would do irreparable harm to an already taxed ocean ecosystem. The SEAL teams were the most logical choice. After all, who knew more about water than us?

These Somali pirate groups had been operating for a while in the Gulf of Aden. Their typical targets were usually smaller transport ships and super yachts. Both were deemed excellent ransom targets. They weren't always pirates though, they started out as a less dangerous, albeit still illegal, group.

After the collapse of the Somali government and the disbanding of the Somali navy these groups started out with illegal fishing. They simply were trying to feed their families. Once local fish stocks were depleted their sights were turned on hijacking personal and commercial vessels.

Many of these vessels, tankers, and small cruise ships were then equipped with water cannons and other security systems. Pirates, apparently, are not stupid and they soon defeated all the defenses. This tanker was the largest threat ever and their location made it more difficult.

What they did not realize was that in the last couple of years their pirate activity had given multiple governments common cause and concern.

There was now a combined task force that included the Indian Navy, Russian Navy, and others. That was who called on us, the Combined Task Force 150. SEALs are known the world over for taking on the most difficult tasks and completing them. We, of course, believed this situation to be no different.

We spent the day reviewing schematics of the ship and, using satellites, tracking the movements of the crew and pirates. It seemed so humorous to me, pirates! All I could see in my mind was a Jack Sparrow type flamboyant sailor as played by Johnny Depp. I wasn't foolish, I DID realize these people were cold blooded killers, but I couldn't get that vision out of my head.

We went over and over the layout of the ship and determined the best way to attack. We would need to start with knives and our bare hands to retain the element of surprise.

In no time we were on a C-17 headed to the area, further planning and strategizing continuing during most of the flight. There was a small naval group sitting far off the coast of Kenya, Southeast of the Gulf of Aden. It was a typical Navy tour of duty thanks to our close ties with Kenya. They would provide good cover for our assault.

By the time we arrived on the ships we were fully prepped and ready to go. We would go in under the cover of darkness using small submersibles. It was too easy for a ship to pick up zodiacs or other surface craft under a bright moon. We also had no idea what they possessed for technology.

When the time arrived, one of the smaller cruisers made a run past the area, about five miles from the ship. They would be somewhat concerned but as the ship zipped past and just kept going the pirates should relax.

They had hostages and were sitting on a massive ecological bomb so likely felt safe. We were advised what they wanted. Their demands included 100 million dollars and two helos to evacuate them and five hostages. Once they were safe in Yemen and out of the immediate area, they would tell us how to disarm the bomb that was set to blow up the ship and split the oil compartments wide open. This was starting to seem less like Somali pirates and more like an international terrorist group. Of course, who it was made no difference to us. We were all about equal opportunity.

The ship slowed enough for us to deploy our submersibles and get loaded. Soon we were all headed towards our target. The silent electric motors whirring in unison, propelling us toward the tanker. Each submersible had a very small buoy tethered to it that rode on the surface of the water and carried multiple HD cameras. We watched the computer screens closely getting views of the sky and 360-degree coverage of the water. Soon enough we could see the outline of the massive tanker ahead of us against the moon-lit horizon.

We prepped and checked our gear one final time. We had one submersible off the starboard bow and the second at the stern of the behemoth. We brought each one almost to the surface and deployed the surface escape hatch. Each sub would send one man up the side of the ship using magnetic handholds.

While they climbed, they would be covered by two operators each from the surface of the water, guns at the ready. They would climb the full distance up the side and once at the top, deploy a rope ladder. The tanker being fully loaded, it was only about a thirty-foot climb. A SEAL can do that with one arm tied behind his (or her!) back and a full pack.

Our coms crackled to life as each team gathered at its end of the ship. With our night vision goggles on it would be easy to spot the invisible to the human eye beacons that marked the hostages.

For the last few years all these large ships were equipped with clothing made with specific thread fibers. When viewed with night vision goggles, they radiated a slight color, almost like the helmet beacons SEALS wore. It made it easy and quick to distinguish friendlies from bad guys.

The other half of the team was going to move to the bridge area to secure the various controls and pumps. Our team was going to where the hostages were being held and ensure their safety. According to overwatch, the hostages appeared to be all held in one room with a couple of sentries outside. We knew we had to secure the hostages and the oil before any weapons were discharged.

The sentries here, at the bow and midships, would have to be taken out almost simultaneously. Two men were assigned to get to where the charges to blow the ship would most likely be located. They were not sophisticated so it was improbable they would have more than one or two blast locations, if they had any at all. Somali pirates and terrorists were solely about cash and used bluffs often.

We communicated quietly on our coms as everyone got in place. We approached the hostage location from two directions. I was less than ten feet from my target.

Each team would have to ensure no guns were fired so it would be critical to disable their trigger hand while taking them out. Keeping them alive was not an issue so that made it somewhat easier.

I heard the comment, on three, in my earpiece and prepared myself.

I left my rifle with Rusty and on "go" I lunged around the corner. His hands carried no weapon as he was busy lighting a cigarette. His rifle was laying against the bulkhead. I assumed because the whole crew was locked up, he wasn't too concerned. I delivered a kick directly to his jaw that drove his head up and back into the steel wall. He was out cold. I had my knife out when Rusty suggested we keep a couple alive. We zip tied his hands and feet tightly, gagged him, removed all his weapons, and opened the hatch.

We told everyone to stay where they were as this was the safest place for them. We closed the hatch door after tossing him and his partner into the room. Fox 1 advised their three were out, Fox 2 said they had eliminated three in the midship area, and we said our two were neutralized. We all heard as overwatch located everyone on our team and let us know there were five people on the bridge. We would need to be careful as one might be the Captain of the ship and there was most likely an operations guy with him.

These tankers were all built the same with the command deck, operations area, and crew quarters at the stern of the ship, stacked in a giant "T" shape.

Getting access to the command deck itself was not a problem as there were many blind spots. The issue would be if they had locked themselves inside or not. There was internal access to the bridge from the crew quarters below and we determined that would be our entrance point. We moved quickly down the ship towards the stern. In no time we were gathered on each side of the bridge structure as well as in the front and rear of it.

Use of weapons wasn't an issue now. There was a maximum of five pirates left but most likely only three. Fox 1 moved close to the side of the bank of windows and used a very tiny camera on the end of a flexible shaft to peek through the window. He described the location of each pirate and the two hostages.

Our task became much easier when he added that the two hostages were white, and the three bogeys were not. When we did breech, each pirate would be targeted by two of us. Again, we needed to act in concert in case there was a bomb. We had already searched the most likely locations and found nothing, but we were in no position to take a chance.

Fox 2 had gained access to the crew quarters along with three others. He advised they were ascending the stairs when we got a break. Our team watched as the bulkhead door creaked slowly open on its rusty hinges as a pirate stepped outside. He left the door ajar as he lit his smoke. Seemingly out of the blue, I watched as his head jerked to the side and he fell to the deck. We cautiously approached him and noticed a growing pool of blood spurting from the knife wound at his jugular.

Whomever had thrown that knife was an absolute star. That was when Boone popped his head around the corner with his finger to his lips. Now there were two left and the door on our side was still open. We told Fox 1 the situation and he told us to go ahead and take them. Two of us took positions on the deck and two waited high.

Rusty threw the door open and in a second there were two dead pirates slumped in their chairs. There wasn't a mark on the Captain or his engineer, other than a little blood spatter on the Captain that came when the Somalis head exploded like a grapefruit. We quickly asked how many pirates the Captain had counted, did the math, and realized there were two more left somewhere. I couldn't see how we had missed anyone but then recalled this is one HUGE ship.

We all immediately scrambled to various areas of the ship hoping there really were no bombs. As we converged in the gangway at the crew quarters, we saw two pirates, securely tied and walking in front of our two guys. They hadn't found any explosives, but they did find these two idiots having a nap. We chuckled about it for a bit and then went to get all the hostages out. They were a little worse for the wear, but nobody was injured badly.

We all gathered on the deck and the Captain advised they were going to continue and finish their voyage. These sailors certainly weren't a wimpy bunch. I kind of admired their resolve. They thanked us profusely with each one of them shaking our hands.

Soon we were back in our submersibles with the ship steaming toward us for retrieval. We had to reload them onto the ship so figured we would have a little race while we waited for them.

We certainly had no intention of leaving million of dollars worth of equipment behind, so we had no choice anyway. We yacked the whole way about how stupid these pirates were and how we would have done it differently if we were them. A dark view of things, but that was often how people in stress filled situations like we lived in responded. You had to joke about it to retain your sanity.

A helo transfer to the air base and we were soon back on US soil and ready to relax. Of course, we had to debrief first with the whole team but that was a necessary evil. We always debriefed when details were fresh as it helped us refine strategies and tactics for future operations. It was also a great opportunity to speak directly with overwatch and team leads and share intel.

For my part, I felt I was settling in well. It was still disconcerting that I was being called Sunny to hide my gender while on coms and that nobody except those in this room knew I was female. I hoped that at some point this would become public knowledge. The SEAL Teams are a bastion of maleness, and it would be great to be known as the one who kicked that door down!

That wasn't the main reason I was here, but it was never far from my mind.

Chapter Thirty 3 – Time Off

As a SEAL, your time off is always dictated by others. World events, your boss, training, threats, whether perceived or real. You never knew when you would be spun up so any liberty that was granted was gratefully accepted. You were also well aware that such time off could end, literally in minutes if a situation arose. Command did try to stagger deployments across teams in an attempt to provide time to recover and recharge, but it wasn't like there was a firm schedule.

Once I was in my vehicle and headed towards home, I decided that I would move into my Aunt's house sooner rather than later. I would drive directly there and have a closer look around. It was on the Balboa Peninsula, not the island and wasn't oceanfront but it was certainly close enough.

It was the smallest house in the area in the middle of 12th Street. The Newport Channel was one direction and Newport Beach, and the Pacific Ocean, was the other direction. The advantage of the house being small was that it had a tree filled yard. 299 – 12th Street was a little oasis in a sea of housing. Long ago, anyone with a lot this size subdivided and built a second house or expanded the original house to what can only be described as stupid-big.

My aunt had never been the type of person who needed to have the largest or most ornate house on a block. She much preferred unique over audacious and character to opulence. That was just who she was. A true woman of substance.

I parked in the garage and walked through the house out to the yard. Once out there it was like you were completely alone. It truly was amazing. This house was one of the very few that had retained the original character of the area. It was all light-colored pastel colors and filled with colorful, hand-made tile on floors and walls.

This house was the definition of "beachy" and I knew I would change as little as possible. As great as the house was and as relaxing as the yard was my favorite spot was the roof top deck. While almost every house and mansion on the peninsula was two stories this house was completed under original building requirements and zoning. Because of that it was almost six feet taller than anything around it, so the rooftop deck had spectacular views of both the channel and the open Pacific. There was not a time when I visited my aunt that we did not sit up on that deck.

It was the perfect place to watch the sun set with the only better location (very slightly better) being out on the sand of Newport Beach itself. I never tired of being here and I knew that when I hung up my rifle that I would retire here.

I awoke refreshed the next day, gave Hector a call and asked if he wanted to pop over. He was blown away when he showed up and shocked when I told him it was mine. He said that he couldn't even afford the property taxes here. I would later find out that neither could I!

We just hung out, cleaned up a bit and had some beers as we talked about all kinds of stuff. We talked for hours with Hector crashing in the guest room that evening.

The next morning, I was emptying things out of my Aunt's dresser when I came across a file simply marked House. I opened it up to find a handwritten note from my aunt. It started out by saying that if I am reading this that she is gone, and I am now the proud owner of this home. She said she always knew that I would be the one to get this place and that I didn't have to worry about anything.

I kept reading as she noted that my name was already on the title so there would be no estate taxes to pay. Then she said I was probably wondering about property taxes, but I needn't worry about that either. She had set up an investment trust that would pay the property taxes each year, for as long as I owned the home. She explained that property taxes that exceeded $1,400.00 per MONTH were just crazy.

I was shocked to find out that the annual taxes for this year were over $15,000.00 and the value of the house was more than $2.3 million.

I was overwhelmed by her gift and thoughtfulness. I wouldn't need a whole lot to live on with no mortgage and no property tax! I went to the kitchen where Hector was cleaning and told him what she had done. I was almost in tears. He smiled and said if I ever needed a roommate, he could be available. We spent the rest of the time loading clothing and things I didn't want to keep out to the garage so we could donate it. I was glad Hector was there to share this with me and provide support.

A few more hours of work and we were pretty much done. I thanked Hector and said I would see him in a few days. I needed to settle in here.

In no time I was back to the gym and even doing a little surfing. The surfing was better at Huntington Beach, so I still found myself there quite often. It seemed everywhere I went I was reminded of my aunt, and it gave me comfort to have those memories. Sometimes it even felt like she was with me as I rode a wave slowly into shore.

I took some time to contemplate my new life as a SEAL. I'm not one to rest on my laurels but I did want to appreciate what I had accomplished.

I got out the box containing my pin and the knife dedicated to Stephen Mills. I recalled eliminating his killer as I held the knife in my hands, feeling a connection to something greater than myself.

Like the trident pin, the weight of the knife seemed to be much heavier than its actual mass. I hoped he knew that I had avenged his death. I hoped they all knew that I had exacted their revenge for them.

Chapter Thirty 4 – My Second Mission as a SEAL

I was in the gym having a great workout when I felt my phone vibrate. The text message was short and simple. It was from Foxtrot 1 and said, 14:00 hours at the armory. I had three hours but with no pets and nobody to notify I could be mobile in no time. I decided to have a nice hot shower at the gym before heading home. As the water cascaded over my head, I wondered what this mission would be? What would my role be? When would I truly become just "one of the guys"?

I zipped home, grabbed a few things, and went to work. I parked my truck and walked double-time to the armory. There was a large table in the center of the building, with all our cages around the perimeter. The table served many functions, but in this case, it was for a small meeting before the main strategy session with the team leads and overwatch. Fox 1 advised there would be a few cake eaters there too so, unfortunately, I would need to remain here until they cleared them out.

I looked at him with a questioning stare and he asked if I had an issue. Rather than whine I suggested that maybe I could attend and pose as an information officer. The Master Chief said he would not lie directly in that manner and added it was too dangerous based on who would be in the room.

Soon they all left without me, and I remained there cleaning and preparing my weapons. I felt a sense of isolation. It felt like I was on the team but at the same time not on the team. I was not impressed.

It wasn't long before Fox 2 returned to the armory to bring me in. As we walked toward the ready room, he apologized for having to do that. I thanked him for his concern and said it was no big deal, that I understood.

I DID understand, but it also really was a big deal for me. I didn't want any kind of special treatment, to be treated any differently than my team-mates. I supposed that I would need to tolerate it for a time and resigned myself to that fact.

As we sat around the table and information such as maps, GPS and other data was being compiled three of the guys quietly said that was a BS move. I felt good that they were concerned and, at least these three, viewed me as one of them. An equal. Just one of the brothers. It was a step in the right direction.

Master Chief Kennedy began to present the details of the operation. Turned out it was another pirate issue, at least that was what it looked like at this point. A super yacht had now been out of touch for two full days and was one day late returning from a charter.

Initially a day late would have been no concern, but we were told there had been contact and a ransom demand.

The information officer brought up a picture of what looked more like a submarine than a yacht. The front half of the craft resembled a submarine with a high deck coming to a point that would easily slice through chop and waves. It swept back smoothly ending 217 feet later at the rear deck. As we looked at the schematic and pictures I was amazed at the size and finish of this craft. It was like nothing I had ever seen. It had not only a hot tub on the rear deck but also a small lap pool. It was 31 feet in the beam so had lots of space inside and out.

The sleek, black hull enclosed six guest cabins for up to 11 guests and crew quarters that housed 17. It could motor all day at 16 knots thanks to two 2,400 HP diesels and travel more than 6,800 miles before requiring refueling. I knew I certainly would NOT want to pay to refuel that thing.

Unfortunately, the fact this was such an advanced yacht would make our task more difficult. There was a heliport as well so it would have all the required radar equipment, in addition to sonar for tracking depths. When the hostage demand was made, we were notified by SECNAV.

Turned out the people being held hostage were personally acquainted with the Secretary of the Navy. That was when we were told that one of the hostages was Jeanie Buss, the President and controlling Owner of the Los Angeles Lakers basketball team. She took over that title when her father, Dr. Jerry Buss passed away. She has a net worth of over $450 million.

We were told she was on this yacht for a test cruise with her brothers Jim and Johnny and their families. I assumed they would have significant security details so the people who perpetrated this kidnapping must be very sophisticated. It was thought they had an inside contact with the company that listed the yacht for sale, but those details really didn't matter.

The safest and most expedient way to save them was for us to get to that boat as quickly as possible. To further attest to the level of expertise of their captors, all the GPS, black box and other equipment that would make the yacht trackable had been disabled. That made them almost invisible, at least electronically invisible.

Our overwatch team had been scouring the ocean in ever growing concentric circles, from their last known location. The yacht had left from Santa Monica and headed almost directly West towards Channel Islands National Park, which is about 73 miles offshore.

The current thinking was they would do one of two things. Either stay close to the coastline where there were hundreds of boats and yachts running up and down the coast or get out past the 200-mile limit into international waters. There was also a third possibility broached by Foxtrot 1 and that would be to motor South and get into Mexican waters. He pointed out that was a little more than 110 miles headed straight South to get to those waters. Cruising at 16 knots, which is about 18 miles per hour, that would take a little more than six hours without accounting for current and winds.

The overwatch team was instructed to scour satellite and other images starting with inlets and small ports inside Mexican waters. Having had at least 48 hours of travel time they could be almost anywhere so the areas being searched were large. Thankfully there was software that would help speed things up exponentially. Using a combination of satellite imagery, naval aircraft and drones, large areas could be searched quickly.

We cooled our jets back at the armory after being told to get fully prepared and rest up. We were not built for sitting and waiting so once all our gear was ready, we broke into small groups. Some of the guys were playing cards, a couple were reviewing new weapons and four of us went to play a little two on two basketball. I think I surprised the guys with my skills. I was certain they had never seen a female ball the way that I could. I also believe it gave them a little more confidence in me. Baby steps.

It wasn't more than three hours later when the yacht was located. They had spotted a few possibilities and re-tasked a satellite to get a closer view. We were already all back in the room when we received confirmation.

The yacht was moored at Loreto on the Eastern side of Baja in the gulf of California. Directly across the gulf was the main body of Mexico, we assumed to provide an easy way for the hijackers to disappear. This would be a difficult location to insert a full team and we did not really wish to be discovered operating in Mexico at the moment. That was when we received a communication from the hijackers.

They had demanded $50 million US in ransom. Clearly, they knew who they had taken and what the family's net worth was. Rather than a direct wire transfer they demanded the money in cash so that bought us an extra day. The bank told them they would need at least 24 hours to get that much cash from the central bank. The bank was told that the cash must be delivered to their location via the Buss family helicopter.

The team had already learned that the family owned a long range Eurocopter. That model could transport six people plus a pilot.

There was no inkling where the cash would be delivered at this point. When they called the next day, they spoke to the Buss family's lawyer who made all the arrangements.

He was told at that time to have the helo fully fueled, including the extra range tanks and the cash loaded in it. We had less than sixteen hours to figure out the best way to handle this.

We had a video call with the lawyer, and he laid out all the details. We didn't advise at that time that we had located the yacht. There was still no intel suggesting an insider, but we could not take chances. It had left the port of Loreto and appeared to be about to round the point at the bottom of Baja and head North up the coast. I found it humorous that these people chose to highjack a yacht in such close proximity to NAB Coronado, the home of the SEAL teams on the West Coast. It felt like a bit of a slap in the face.

We decided that three of our team would rush immediately to John Wayne Airport where the Buss copter was sitting. There were a couple of places to hide within the craft so that we would not be seen until it landed on the yacht or wherever it was told to land. It turned out that Boone was a licensed helo pilot, so he was one of the people selected. Fox 2 and me were the other two. I had already proven myself lethal in close quarters and hand to hand combat, so I felt I was a good choice.

We loaded up our gear and quickly headed North to John Wayne. The rest of the team continued to track the yacht as the team gathered its weapons, chutes, and water gear. Preparedness, as always, was the key to success.

As we drove, we were informed the yacht was still heading North and the lawyer had confirmed that Jeanie Buss, her brothers, and families were still on the yacht. Without continuing proof of life, the hijackers would never see the cash.

In many cases like this even if the cash is delivered the hostages still end up dead. Using a SEAL team gave the families a much greater chance of survival. The rest of the team was already in the air so they could parachute down ahead of the line of travel of the yacht if necessary.

We arrived at the airport ready to go. The cash got there about two hours after we did, packed into large black duffel bags. The lawyer had been advised the cash was to be packed into these bags, placed into a secure cargo net, and hanging beneath the helo. When it arrived at the boat it would receive further instructions.

The pilot seemed anxious but not what you would call nervous. Turned out he was way more than basic qualified. He had been an army pilot with multiple tours in Iraq and Afghanistan. We tried to substitute Boone for him, but he insisted he was up to the task. He watched closely as we loaded all our weapons, checked clips and secured knives. The only way to be successful was the element of surprise and a quick, aggressive attack as soon as they were in range.

We assumed they would attempt to take the helicopter along with Jeanie Buss to ensure their getaway. Soon we were in motion and moving quickly over the Pacific headed South. Overwatch let us know the yacht was still moving Northbound, almost 100 miles off the coast. We headed to the GPS coordinates that had been provided and watched as the yacht headed towards our location.

As we hovered, we saw three high speed offshore race boats heading towards the same spot. They were either planning to all go different directions or this was some sort of ruse to throw us off. As the helo began to drop toward the helipad on the yacht its short-range radio crackled open. They told him to first drop the bag and then land the craft, leaving the motor on. Any tricks and everyone would be shot.

The three of us crouched low hidden by the front seats and the one-way windows. Fox 2 was on one side and Boone and I were on the other. The pilot whispered two left, one right so I slid over next to Fox 2. The far door opened, and Boone drove a knife deep into the hijacker's throat. The pilot said the deck was clear so when our door slid open, we each lunged at our man.

Grabbing their rifles and twisting them out of their hands they were down and out quickly.

In a matter of seconds, one was dead, and two others were securely tied up face down on the deck. As the deck of the yacht was almost 25 feet from the surface of the ocean the people in the speedboats could not see what was happening.

According to overwatch, it had appeared that only three people had hijacked the yacht. They had already confirmed with the lawyer exactly how many adults and children were there and had done the math.

We were confident there were no more threats on the boat. As we went to peek over the port and starboard to get the lay of the land, I spotted two men approaching from the stern. Thank God for great peripheral vision. I raised my rifle, quickly determining they also had weapons and with two squeezes of the trigger they were both down.

I could not be positive they were part of the criminal group so had taken non-lethal shots on both. Boone and I moved quickly to check and disarm them as the other two boats roared off. The massive HP in those things got them moving very quickly but one not too quick for Fox 2.

I heard his weapon discharge twice and then heard a loud boom and saw a massive plume of black smoke rising into the air. There was no more boat, and we were positive anyone on board had met their maker.

We chuckled as the other one cut its engines and just floated along with their hands up in the air. We knew they weren't going anywhere so we quickly searched the boat and thankfully found everyone confined to one stateroom. Other than a couple of kids crying, they were no worse for the wear it appeared.

Fox 2 and Boone got everyone out as I took care of the two on the back of the boat. Within minutes, two offshore boats roared up to the back of the yacht. It was more of our team, so we let them know we had everything under control. The pilot knew I was a woman, but he was the only one. The hostages only saw me with helmet and goggles on. I jumped into the first boat and waited for Fox 2 and Boone. They confirmed everyone was okay and there was enough fuel to get them home and that was it.

The helo pilot had asked Fox 2 if we wanted a ride back, but he said the boats would work fine. He also let him know to keep it a secret that he had seen a female SEAL operator. It was classified and he wouldn't want to tell anyone about it. They shook hands, shared a HooYah and that was that.

Soon we were all skimming over the waves back towards Coronado with an extra boat and five bad guys. It was a unique operation, and I was surprised that SECNAV would use a team in this way. Although, based on what I had done before officially becoming a SEAL, I was certain it was not the first time.

Chapter Thirty 5 – Home Sweet Home

After being debriefed, I was excited to get back to my Aunt's, oops, my house. The boys had other plans however and soon we were tipping a few beers at McP's Irish Pub & grill, a famous SEAL hangout close to the base. We were all dressed in civvies, so it wasn't like I was going to be discovered or anything. Master Chief Kennedy encouraged me to stick with the team, so I did.

McP's had been in the news recently as the location where Chris Kyle (American Sniper) had supposedly punched out former governor Jesse Ventura. The story goes that Ventura said a few not so flattering things about George W Bush and the SEALs. The SEALs were gathered for a wake in honor of Michael Monsoor, a SEAL who had been killed in Iraq in 2006.

Kyle wasn't a man who tolerated people badmouthing Dubya or the SEALs, so he decked the guy he called scruff face. Ventura launched a lawsuit that appears to be fizzling out as, even though Chris Kyle died tragically and the suit continued, defense witnesses have continued to stack up claiming that Ventura started the scrap.

McP's was created by an original SEAL Team 1 guy, Greg McPartlin. After three tours in Vietnam, he figured he and his brothers needed a place to relax. It has been a SEAL hangout ever since. I was looking forward to someday being able to let it be known that I really WAS a SEAL and not just a hang-around.

We had a pretty quiet night, nobody getting into any trouble, and soon I was headed to my house. It was only 90 miles up I-5 to Newport but it seemed to take forever, even at 80 miles an hour. I just wanted to get home, maybe soak in a tub, or just sit up on the roof deck. I would decide when I arrived. I pulled into the garage as the sun was beginning to set and decided I need to go directly to the roof.

I grabbed a bottle of wine, put on some flip flops, and went up the stairs. I was very happy the sun wasn't completely down yet. I watched the bronze hued mist spinning off the tops of the breaking waves swirling like snow blowing off a remote mountaintop. I was glad I was close enough to be able to hear the waves as they compressed and then crashed down to foam and rolled gently up onto the sand. It was one of the most relaxing sounds in the world to me. I wasn't going to have too much wine as I wanted a good beach run in the morning to start my day.

My eyes opened to see nothing but stars as I was curled up underneath a blanket.

I glanced at my watch and when I saw it was now 1:30 AM I decided to stay right where I was. I flattened out the chaise completely, grabbed a second blanket and drifted blissfully off to sleep. The mesmerizing sounds of the ocean and a slight breeze like a lullaby in my head.

The sun was up and already beating down on me when a distant car alarm woke me from my slumber. I was really out. I went inside, grabbed a yogurt, and returned to my spot. After I was done, I did a little limbering up and stretching and then went downstairs, grabbed my runners, and hit the beach.

I could run up and down that coast all day long it seemed, never tiring of the sound of the surf. It was already getting warm, and I was thankful I was just wearing a running top and short compression shorts. Every now and then I would dip down to the firm sand letting the mist from the ocean cool me off.

The sun began heating up my now salty face and body as I ran and ran and ran. I had long been in the zone where I could go seemingly forever, my body and mind in perfect synch. Running was effortless for me once I hit that point. At times it was like I was gliding over the sand and asphalt rather than running on it. An ethereal being who no one could see as I floated past them.

Just as I was ready to head back, I heard a woman scream that someone had taken her purse. I followed the sound of her voice and saw someone in a dark hoody running away with a purse under his arm. He was headed towards the main street, running away from the beach. I couldn't resist so I took chase. As I ran past the woman, I told her to stay there, I would be right back.

I picked up the pace and saw him turn into an alley behind the small shopping mall. As I rounded the corner he had stopped and had the purse open, rooting through it for cash. I told him to drop the purse and whatever he had already taken, and I would let him go. He looked at me, laughed, and told me to mind my own business. I walked slowly toward him and told him once more that he didn't want this kind of trouble. I asked him to please give me the purse, adding I didn't want anyone to get hurt here.

He threw it at my face as he moved toward me. He made a feeble attempt to punch me, which I easily slipped. He said something about one more chance before he gets serious, and I tagged him one right on the nose before he finished talking.

It was just a quick, but firm, blow to get some blood going and prove to him he should stop.

He took a stance like a boxer would and asked me to give it my best shot. He was not prepared for me to fake a punch but at the last moment deliver a direct close-range kick to the head. I snapped my leg out like a whip, following through to ensure solid contact. I could see he was both dazed by the blow and shocked that I could do it. I really hoped he would just stop but when he came at me again, I had no choice.

As he tried to punch me in the head I moved sideways and took control of his arm. I took him down to the ground where he was now face first on the asphalt my knee deep into his back and his arm twisted up high.

He couldn't move and started yakking about police brutality. Just as I yelled at him, I wasn't a cop, I heard a voice behind me saying, "but I am." I kept control and turned to see two uniformed officers smiling down at me.

The male officer looked at me and said I suppose this is the clown who snatched that lady's purse? I said I saw him do it and when I caught up to him, he attacked me. The officer smiled and said it appeared that was his second mistake of the day? He said they would take over from here, so they grabbed him and cuffed him.

His partner took the guy to the car while he told me citizens shouldn't get involved in this kind of thing, it was very dangerous etc etc. I just chuckled and said the crook was the only one in any danger here today. He looked at me, smiled and said he supposed that was the case based on how the purse snatcher looked. He took my name and number in case I was needed in court and then I grabbed the purse and everything and took it back to the lady.

I just smiled, told her I said I would be back, and handed it over to her with a have a nice day. As I ran back to my place, I decided I wouldn't mind being a cop. I was certain I couldn't stand the monotony or sticking to ALL the rules, but it was nice to help someone like that. And nobody had to die for a change. I knew in my heart the work I was doing was the right thing but killing people weighs on you, even if they ARE bad people.

Over the next few weeks, I hung out with Hector quite a bit, stuck to my training schedule and did a lot of running and surfing. I really wasn't good at surfing, but I liked the way it felt. Skimming over the waves with the sun warming me up, my legs absorbing the shocks and trying to stay upright. It was both an adrenaline rush and super-relaxing at the same time. I finished up surfing and laid on my towel until I dried off and then headed home.

The surfing at Newport wasn't the best but then I could simply walk to and from the sand so that made up for it.

I didn't really hear too much from the guys after we split so I was a little surprised when I got a text from Boone. He said they were surprising Fox 1 with a birthday party over at Magic's place. He lived over in Garden Grove and had a yard large enough for this size party. I said that was a great idea, I would be there.

It was a BBQ type affair and when I arrived about ¾ of the team was already there. As I glanced around, I noticed most all of them seemed to have a plus one. I never considered that I should, or could, bring a date. Then again, this was my first real team event outside of a bar or a firefight who would I bring anyway?

Boone came up to greet me with one of the other guys and then Magic came over. They all said it was great I was able to come over with me answering why wouldn't I? Soon I had a cold beer in my hand, and I was being introduced to various wives and girlfriends.

Most had the same comments either telling me to keep their clown husbands/boyfriends out of trouble or congratulating me for representing our gender on the teams. All of them agreed it was about time! Most adding they certainly couldn't do it.

Nevertheless, it felt like they were looking at me like something I was not. I wasn't their mother, their babysitter or anything close to that. I was their equal, an operator, a highly trained and very skilled member of a highly trained and very skilled team. Oddly, this was the first time I felt like I was somehow not the equal of the men on my team and the feeling was coming from the females in their lives. This wasn't at all what I was expecting.

It seems we women struggle sometimes with envy coloring our thoughts and opinions about one another. That was something else I thought we were past, but I suppose we simply were not there yet. Hopefully, in time that would change. I knew that nobody on the teams shared details about operations though so I wondered how the boys would be able to share that I was as good (or better) than they were.

As the party wore on, it became clear to me that we were all perhaps getting a little shack wacky. After all, SEALs function best when challenged to the maximum of their ability and then some. You couldn't stay sharp by training only. We needed to be living on the edge. A few of the guys had perhaps a little too much to drink and I decided I would take off before things got strange. You never truly knew what might happen when SEALs were mixed with a healthy dose of alcohol.

I wished Master Chief Kennedy a great birthday, let Magic know I was leaving and then Boone walked with me to the gate.

He said he hoped we were on an op soon and I agreed wholeheartedly as the gate swung closed behind me.

Chapter Thirty 6 – Iran

While the yacht rescue was interesting it was not what one would refer to as a "typical" SEAL operation. Almost everything we did was in secrecy and almost everything was outside of the continental USA. That operation had neither of those qualities.

While SEAL Team 6 got all the notoriety, unwanted I am sure, the teams were all relatively similar. They were certainly structured the same. However, it seemed to me that ST 7 now had a chip on its shoulder. Having two leaders and other key people relieved of their duties put a bit of target on the teams back so everything was scrutinized just a little more. I think the lead officers wanted (perhaps needed) a big win, like ST 6 got with Bin Laden. I already believed that Foxtrot team within ST 7 was the platoon they felt could deliver.

Finally, the call came. I received the now usual simple text, Armory at 06:00, and I knew we would soon be off. I had the evening to prepare the house and get things closed up and at 04:30 I was off to Coronado. Soon we were all seated around the table in the ready room listening intently to the Master Chief lay out where we were headed and what we would be doing.

We were going to Shindand Air Base in Western Afghanistan. It was about halfway between the North and South borders almost directly West of Kabul close to the border with Iran.

We were told that for what we would be doing, although Bagram was better equipped, Shindand was easier to stay off the radar. The mission was extremely important to US interests in that area of the world. Then again, ALL SEAL team missions are extremely important.

Iran had been on our nuclear radar for quite a few years but with recent proliferation of nuclear devices we were going to do some inspections. Top secret inspections of course, but inspections, nevertheless. While drones, high flying spy aircraft and satellites provided the US with some intel we were now at a time that required closeup eyes on the prize.

Official inspections were not going to cut it as it gave them the chance to show only what they wanted. We would need more widespread coverage. We would have to get eyes deep into the country precisely where they did not want us to look. Those eyes would belong to us, the Fox platoon of ST 7. With Iran removing its own restrictions on nuclear production, it was imperative that we find out exactly what was going on.

There was also a secondary part of this mission. Once we had gathered all the required intel and mapped out each location and what was there, we needed to shed light on the subject. To do so, it had been decided that we would initiate a sizable explosion at one of the sites. It absolutely had to look like an accident so we could leave no footprint.

When we blew the site, we could not shoot any weapons or leave any dead bodies behind. At least not bodies that could be autopsied after such a blast. Such an explosion would register on many other countries radar and satellite tracking systems. The US and other countries could then demand increased transparency in the region.

The location would need to be as far as possible from any of the ones that were currently being inspected. This would provide proof that Iran was not being completely up front about their arsenal. The world would then have a moral obligation to complete further inspections and perhaps implement additional embargoes and sanctions.

We all watched closely as a schematic of an ICBM was put on the screen. There was screen after screen of detail, the last one showing a fuel line that could be sabotaged. An explosion resulting from this area would leave absolutely no trace of what had happened. The only accelerant needed would be the rocket fuel itself.

It would look exactly like a malfunction which would help the US and its allies make the case on the global stage that Iran was a bigger problem than anyone thought. Not only were they secretly building more nuclear weapons, and rockets to deliver them, but they also lacked skill in the area of safety.

This would be an extremely challenging operation. Everything must be done at night. We would absolutely need to be back on base before nightfall or have somewhere to lay low during the day. It would also be crucial to leave as few bodies behind as possible.

In addition, the explosion would have to be timed for when we were completely clear of the area and safely back on base. It would require a longer than typical delay and fuse setup which poses its own challenges. The trigger could be accidentally found before the explosion, which would compromise everything we were trying to accomplish.

We had originally expected to pose as Iranian insurgents, maybe the Baluch. The only issue was that they confined their efforts to Eastern Iran. As Sunnis in a predominantly Shiite country, that may make things difficult if we were too far from that area. Overland travel would be even more challenging.

It was determined that the best choice would be to act as Taliban. While the Taliban did not run around attacking Iranians, they frequently used Iran to hide. If we did run into any issues, we would need to be surgical and leave as few traces as possible. Also, due to the secrecy of our mission we could easily be mistaken by US or Afghan forces as real Taliban. That would be a real and present danger for us and one we would need to be cognizant of at all times.

We got into much greater detail once we boarded the aircraft to head to Shindand. It was another of the Army's C 17's that was transporting supplies and ordnance, so we just hitched a ride. It was more than a twenty-hour flight and we didn't get much sleep. Two hours after landing we were fully geared up and ready to go.

We had local vehicles at our disposal with multiple places to hide both people and weapons. Although travelling at night offered a certain amount of cover, it also made you stand out at times. We had GPS coordinates of the five sites that we needed to get to. Once there, we would use various pieces of sensitive equipment to determine the presence of nuclear materials.

The landscape would not be traversed easily. The sandy hills were difficult to climb and there were few places to hide.

We already knew that hiding in plain sight was dangerous but also most likely the best option in this case. People anywhere didn't usually approach Taliban to see how things were going.

Not only did we need to determine the presence of nuclear weapons, but we would also need to find out if there were ICBMs at those sites capable of delivering such a payload. Generally, Iran did not have sophisticated and covert missile silos like the US did so we were hoping that part might not be too difficult.

As darkness crept its way across the landscape, we set out in four vehicles. Overwatch would keep us posted about any oncoming vehicles so we could divert off the road or path and get behind cover. Avoiding detection would be our most important task for the next few days.

There were four of us in our vehicle and, based on the banter, I was feeling like this really was a home for me. I KNEW that I was safe, and that team goals and SEAL promises would conquer all else.

It was good to be just another operator for a change. I had my team to rely on and they relied on me. I think I preferred this to being a lone wolf.

It was not just the camaraderie, it was the sense of team, family, and common purpose. Hopefully, I was finally just one of the boys.

Who would have thought the toughest, most highly trained, and macho group on the planet would seemingly easily accept a female in their midst? As an equal too! I suppose my performance thus far had earned me that respect, but I expected it to be given grudgingly.

We talked about everything under the sun as we drove through the black night over dunes and difficult terrain. After two hours of navigating rough and rocky terrain we were within three miles of our first location.

Overwatch had advised there could be nuclear weapons at the site, but we had to get inside to confirm. We were also hoping that there would be ICBM's too as this would be the easiest location from which to escape unscathed after we rigged an explosion.

We hid the vehicles under some camo nets and went the rest of the way on foot. At what would be considered a light jog we covered the ground quickly and were soon scanning the fenced off area for possible access points. We noted the location and timing of sentries, and it quickly became obvious they felt quite safe in this location.

The sentries appeared a little lackadaisical about their job and the enormous responsibility of protecting nuclear weapons. Other than the razor wire topped high fence, there was little to deter unwanted entry it seemed. Although we were dressed as Taliban fighters, we retained our reflective undergarments. They prevented infra red and heat sensing cameras from picking up a signature so we were rendered virtually invisible to most of the technology they would be using. We also had minimal weaponry with us and would rely on hand-to-hand, knives and perhaps the garotte I had slipped into my pocket if we were confronted.

Unless we got too close to the lights, or the sun rose, there was little opportunity for us to be detected. We decided to set up posts around the perimeter with only two of us designated to enter the facility. Boone and Rusty were the ones selected to go. The rest of us positioned ourselves to be able to maintain eye contact with each other.

It did not take them long to peruse the facility, they were back outside the fence within fifteen minutes. They must have been motoring to cover that much ground so fast.

We got back to our vehicles and as we headed to our next target.
We were advised there were ICBM`s on that site as well as what appeared to be nuclear bombs, or at least nuclear materials to make a bomb. The good thing about an explosion like we were planning is

there was very little possibility of a nuclear event occurring. Nuclear bombs simply did not work that way.

A nuclear bomb did not work like regular explosive. In a nuclear device it is nuclear fission that creates the destructive power. Basically a "bullet" of Uranium 235 is fired towards a central mass of the material. When the neutron pierces the atom there it creates a massive chain reaction where in parts of milliseconds additional neutrons are created that then explode another atom.

That process all happens in a split second and the nuclear device explodes. There are three critical and very damaging and destructive things that follow. There is a wave of intense heat, a massive blast of pressure that can level buildings, and then the radiation and radioactive fallout.

The heat at ground zero, or the hypocenter, of the blast can approach 500 million degrees Fahrenheit, vaporizing everything close to it. The damage from these weapons is beyond description and long-lasting, something the world needs to avoid. That was why this mission was so important.

We made our way quickly through the rocky terrain to the next location. In about the same amount of time we were able to confirm the presence of a nuclear bomb lab. In virtually no time at all we were headed back to Shindand. It had been decided that we would complete the first two inspections and then confirm next steps back at the base.

We rolled through the gates long before the sun rose and were sitting in the ready room debriefing when the ST 7 XO entered the room. In atypical fashion, at least for SEALs, everyone jumped to attention. We were told to be seated and the XO went over the details with us.

Although we had all been trained in demolition and explosives the XO looked directly at Fresh and asked if he could pull it off? Yes sir, he barked out followed by a HooYah. The XO looked at Fox 1 and simply said, lay it out for them Master Chief Kennedy. As he walked past him on his way out, I watched him whisper a "don`t let me down, Art" on his way past the Master Chief.

Clearly there was much more than we knew riding on this operation. Boone elbowed me in the ribs as he saw the exchange too. We completed reviewing all the details of the two facilities and transitioned to discussing the locations and challenges of the next three. We were told that the first location would indeed be the one where we would rig the explosion and that mission would be carried out in three days.

We now had GPS coordinates of the other three installations and got into planning our route. The mountainous and rough terrain would again present some challenges but, after all, we are SEALs so there was no real concern. Of course, we knew this wasn't a walk in the park and we always knew the dangers, but we were confident.

Confidence, bravery, and commitment were all deeply ingrained in every SEAL and that held true for our team too.

We relaxed outside with a couple beers each and then had a good meal before getting some rack time. I was certainly ready to sleep but didn't really require it. All of us could operate, at full readiness and capacity, with almost no sleep. It was part of who we were now.

Chapter Thirty 7 - Contact

As the sun began to set slowly over the horizon, we completed our preparations. We were headed to the farthest target from the base and there was a very real possibility we would need to hunker down for the day somewhere out there. The route took us past mountainous areas where one would expect to find caves that would provide us cover.

We got into the vehicles and began driving. We drove for over five hours before pulling the vehicles off the road/path and taking a bit of a break. Bio breaks and snacks were in order and, once completed, we resumed our trek. Approximately two hours before the destination, we spotted some caves that would be our most likely hiding place. Sitting in a cave is not usually how one would like to spend 12 or 13 hours, but we had little choice.

We motored on and again pulled the vehicles off and hid them about three miles from the target. We covered them with the camo tarps, grabbed our gear and did another slow jog through the sandy and rocky terrain. As we crested a hill, we noted that this was the largest instalment we had seen thus far. Searching it would neither happen in fifteen minutes nor would it take only two people to accomplish.

It was going to be very helpful that overwatch had provided us with a site layout. It highlighted the best places to search first so that would simplify our task and reduce our time on target. Nevertheless, we would need at least four people, if not six, to complete the inspection quickly. That would be crucial to exiting undetected with the information we needed. We made our plan and decided who was going where and cautiously entered the facility.

This time I was with Magic as we went to a location where we could safely breech the fence. If we couldn't climb it undetected then we would cut a small hole that we could easily patch after we got in and again when we left. We would only require this to be undiscovered for two days as once the other facility was blown to kingdom come, all investigation would be focused there.

We cut our way through the fence, tied it back up with the same wire and moved silently through the compound. Although we were 100% ready, we definitely did not want to encounter anyone. We located what we were after, painted it with invisible to the naked eye trackable material and were back outside the fence in less than 25 minutes. We met back up with the rest of the team at about the same time and began to move away from the site.

We got back to our vehicles, stored all the camo tarps, and started our drive to the caves. After a little less than two hours, and almost a full hour before sunrise, we were safely entrenched in the caves, our vehicles once again hidden by tarps. We had set up a watch system so that we could sleep in small groups deep inside the back of the cave.

Sentries remained outside on high ground, maintaining contact with overwatch to ensure we did not get surprised. I was on sentry, shortly before sunrise, when a soft voice crackled in my earpiece. It advised there were five heat signatures that appeared to be moving toward our location. It could be anyone, but we needed to be extra cautious here.

It might be real Taliban, Iranian farmers or an Iranian family simply moving around when it was safer to do so. We would have no way of knowing until they were close to us. We kept an eagle eye out and then finally saw the small group. Through my spotting scope I could see they were armed, and they did not appear to be Americans. Of course, we were armed and had nothing to identify us as Americans either.

We readied ourselves and took up positions that would allow us to get close and neutralize them if required. As the group rounded a large rock outcropping close to us, they appeared to assume a military position. A lead person, one in the rear and three together in the middle. Fox 1 told me to get the rear guy once they resumed moving ahead.

Once they were past, I snuck up on him, quickly got him into a choke hold and subdued him. We knew there would not be much time before this was noticed so the rest of the team converged quickly.

Luckily there were no shots fired and the skirmish ended quickly. We had all five captured, gagged and secured but now we had a bigger problem. They were Iranian nationals but did not appear to be military after all. They were armed and travelling at night though, so it was difficult to determine what they were. We could not simply take them back to the base as if it was discovered that we had taken Iranian citizens hostage that would not end well.

We met in the front of the cave as the sun rose to discuss. That was when Magic and the Master Chief said they would take care of the matter. They told us to stay put and hold down the fort, they would return soon. They told us they were going to take them all over the hill and release them, telling them if they wanted to live, they would not say a word to anyone. I felt that something else was going to happen but said nothing to anyone.

There was little doubt that had they have gotten the drop on us they would have attacked. They were armed and appeared ready to fight. They were dressed like insurgents or thieves. In my heart, I knew that Fox 1 and 2 were going to take them out and kill them but I didn't want to think about it.

SEALs may be assassins from time to time, but we are not murderers...at least as far as I knew.

They came back to the caves, and we went over the planning for the explosion to be staged at the first location. We would be able to check out the other two locations on the way back to camp once nightfall arrived. After that, we would spend the next evening creating the conditions for the ICBM explosion.

Fresh, our other explosives expert, seemed to enjoy telling us about the various combustibles and fuels used in these rockets. His real name was Darcy, but we had only known him as Fresh. He seemed like a bit of a pretty boy if you asked me, but still one heck of a SEAL.

The main difference between liquid fuel and solid was that liquid fuel was ignited in a combustion chamber and could be controlled. You could moderate the fuel flow to the chamber to control speed and trajectory of a rocket.

Solid fuel on the other hand, once ignited, cannot be turned off or regulated. It's kind of like a bomb. The fuel (such as acrylic acid/aluminum powder) and the oxidizer (usually ammonium perchlorate) are solidified into a mass using a binder. When it ignites, it burns at 100% and does not stop until it is completely used up.

Lucky for us these were liquid fueled rockets. That would make an "accidental" explosion much easier to sell. Fresh advised that he would require a maximum of ten minutes on task to rig everything. He didn't go into much detail but told us that basically he was going to route the fuel flow back onto itself. A small, perfectly placed charge would ignite it at just the right time. This would make for a massive explosion and complete destruction of the trigger mechanism he was building as well as everything within 200 yards of the blast.

A day later we were safely back in camp and reviewing the details of our sortie to the initial location. Fresh had the mechanism he would use along with a back up that he would also install. They were both packed away in bubble wrap inside his pack and we settled in for the day. I hated waiting around like this, I found it very difficult to be idle for that length of time. I went over to sit with Darcy for a bit and find out a bit about him.

He was quite free with the information explaining that he had always been a munitions and bomb expert. He was one of those kids who was never without a chemistry set and started blowing things up in grade school. He asked me about my background and wondered how I got into the SEALs. I just smiled and said the same way everyone else did except I was top of the class!

He nodded, knowingly it seemed, and went on to tell me about his own sister. She had been a police officer who had been killed in action. He added that he thought she could have made a great SEAL, but it was too difficult ten years ago. I grinned and told him it was still difficult and that was where the conversation ended. I wanted to get a little shuteye before we had to begin getting prepared.

The good thing about this part of the operation is that taking a few people out would not be an issue. Once that missile blew, most of the installation would be a wasteland leaving almost no evidence behind. The explosion would be large enough to register on various countries monitoring stations and that would prompt a deeper inspection in Iran. They had been keeping all inspections out of this section of the country, but they could not hide an incident of this size from the world.

Once everyone was gathered, we mapped out our plan and discussed options and possible pinch-points. Fox 1 said we would need two snipers to remain on high ground and he said that would be me and Boone. Everyone else was given tasks with Magic and Rusty planning to move with Fresh to cover him while he rigged the ICBM to blow.

As the whole mechanism would be hidden, and there would be no reason for anyone to look at that part of the missile, he could set the delay to whatever was needed.

We wanted to be back on base and perhaps even on an aircraft out before the explosion, so the time delay would be five hours. In no time we were again trekking over the rocky terrain approaching our target.

When we got within about 1,000 yards Fox 1 pointed at one hill for Boone and another, across the valley for me. I trudged up the hill with my weapon and got set up on a small ridge, just below the peak. It would keep me well hidden and even if I fired, very difficult to locate.

I pulled on my ghillie suit, set up my rifle and began to scan the area with my spotting scope. A Ghillie suit looked a lot like a shrub. Once you were in it and prone it was extremely difficult for anyone to locate you, especially from a thousand or so yards away. I watched closely as they approached the fence and cut a section open. All together, five of them entered, leaving four more outside the fence. Now it was a matter of keeping our eyes peeled and waiting for them to emerge again.

It seemed like forever, but in less than thirty minutes I watched them leave through the same hole in the fence and re-secure it. Once they were clear of the facility we gathered back together as a team and moved quickly to our vehicles.

Not a shot fired and not one man had to be taken out.

Either we were just that good or the Iranians were clueless in keeping something secure. It didn't matter to us, as we were soon to board a plane and leave Afghanistan.

THE FIRST FEMALE NAVY SEAL

We were all sitting in the rear of the Globemaster aircraft and as it banked left Fresh called me over next to him. We looked out the window and he began to count down. He said three, two one and as he said boom, we could see a large plume of thick black smoke spinning up into the sky from inside Iran. He just smiled and said, right on time. That was that.

By the time we were being debriefed back at Coronado the word had already gotten out. The US and other countries were wanting better access to Iran and trade embargoes were already increasing. Our XO came in and congratulated Fox 1 on getting it done, he was glad he had made the right choice.

After he left it was business as usual. We discussed equipment, weapons, overwatch and what we might improve on. We had a few laughs about army aircraft and the lack of flight attendants and then went our separate ways.

In what would rapidly become a habit for me I was soon fast asleep under blankets on my rooftop patio. As much as I loved being with the guys and doing my job, I really enjoyed my alone time.

I could look at the stars for hours on end and never tire of it.

I enjoyed finding the various constellations and identifying the main stars in each. I would often make trips to the Griffith Observatory just to look at the whole Los Angeles basin lit up.

It was like there were a million stars above me and a million stars below when I was up there. I loved that place; it was just SO L.A.

Chapter Thirty 8 – Beach Life

Now that I was fully moved into my Aunt's house, I was really enjoying beach life. There was something about waking up on that roof that made life seem perfect. The air was always fresh and clean, with just the right amount of ocean smell. The sun seemed to shine almost every day, warming my face as I awoke.

I decided I needed to install a coffee station up there and maybe a little bar too. I always felt completely safe and secure with not a worry in the world when I was on that roof. It had become my own little fortress of solitude. Sometimes I felt like I never wanted to leave it.

I went downstairs, put on some shorts and a top and went for a long walk along the water. You could walk, or run, for miles along that coastline. I liked that I fit in there and was just another girl with a ponytail and ball cap walking the beach. I would get the odd second look, but nobody really bothered me when I was out here. That was one of the best things about Southern California, everyone just more or less did their own thing.

I went home and sat in the back yard to have some lunch. This was another perfect spot and great feature of this house.

You couldn't see other houses or the street and the only clue that you weren't deep in the forest was the odd traffic sound. I enjoyed a leisurely lunch and then decided I needed a workout. I relaxed for a bit after eating and then went to the gym.

I loved the gym. I was always challenging myself to lift more and train harder. I didn't waste time when I was working out either and had no tolerance for those who did. Sometimes it would make me seem anti-social but if someone wanted to take the time to know me, they would see that wasn't the case at all. I could be a very social person and very engaging...when I wanted to be!

I was just finishing a set of heavy squats when I heard a familiar voice. It was Hector asking where the hell I had been. I told him I was out of town on business and went back to finish my fourth set. He waited until I was done, and he asked if I wanted to hit Fred's in Huntington Beach for some food and a margarita or two tonight. I said that sounded like a great idea and we agreed to meet there around 7:00.

I took my time finishing up and cooling down and then went home for a little nap. I awoke feeling refreshed a couple of hours later. I had another shower, put on some jeans and a sweatshirt, and jumped in my car.

I drove up the Pacific Coast Highway, enjoying the drive as always, and was at Fred's in no time. Their address was on the PCH, but the entrance was off Main Street, so I parked around the corner. I ran into Hector just as I started up the wide tiled staircase. Before we got to the top, he spotted the hostess and asked if there was a table on the rail left. She smiled at him like she knew him, nodded, and asked us to follow her.

We had a table right against the outside railing of the narrow patio looking over the Huntington Beach Pier and the Pac Highway.

It was the perfect spot from which to watch the sun set and that was exactly what we were going to do.

I asked Hector if he knew the hostess and he admitted it was his little sister. She had worked here for three years now and, more or less, ran the wait staff. He had called ahead, and she saved us the table.

I smiled at him and said, this isn't a date, is it? He laughed, a little too hard, and said not in a million years. He would never date a woman who could kick his ass. I decided to believe him and truly hoped that we could remain simply friends. I laughed along with him and said I wouldn't want to date a guy whose ass I could kick anyway. He grinned at me and said that must make for a pretty shallow dating pool. True enough I responded.

We enjoyed some chips with Fred`s homemade salsa and a margarita to start things off. This was one of those spots where I could sit for hours. Between people watching and seeing the plethora of classic cars rolling buy on the PCH it was a perfect place for me. It seemed every night was "cruise night" when you were at Fred's in the evenings. I recalled going to Colorado Boulevard in Pasadena for cruise nights when I was in high school, before we moved to Boston.

A seemingly endless parade of cars snaking their way down Colorado at about four miles an hour. You could see everything from stock supercars to original classics with a good dose of all kinds of customs mixed in. Some of the low riders had paint jobs like I had never seen in my life with detail that would floor even the best artist.We quickly returned to people watching looking at singles and couples going to and from the pier and then walking up or down the Pac Highway.

We would pick out a couple and decide what their story was. We believed some were cheating on their partners based on how they acted together and how they walked. No hand holding or arms around one another to give them away. It would also offer plausible deniability, a term I was becoming very familiar with in my work life, should they be spotted.

We sat and talked for hours and marvelled at the sunset as it lit up the sky in hues of colors you simply didn't see anywhere else.

Gold beams of light glinting off the tops of the small waves as they rolled towards their foamy demise on the sand. Each wave unique, starting and ending at different spots from the one before and the one after. That's what I found in surfing too. Like snowflakes, there were never two waves alike. That was one of the things that made surfing fun, variety. Variety was also what made my job interesting.

We went our separate ways after the sun was down and on my drive home, I continued to contemplate my job. One day I would be rescuing crew and hostages from a tanker, the next I might be spying in a hostile country and the day after would bring another unique adventure.

Of course, for most people, an adventure doesn't usually include a risk of death but that was what I had signed up for. The good and the bad.

Chapter Thirty 9 – Baghdad

The bombing and attack of the US Embassy in Baghdad would have to be considered one of the bad days of my job. The US Embassy in Iraq was hit with multiple rockets attributed to Iranian nationals. The Iran-Iraq conflict has been ongoing for many years but this attack on a US embassy was of particular to concern to our government.

Almost immediately we were in the air and headed to Iraq, discussing the situation at length during the flight. What we were being told was in direct opposition to what was coming out of the white house via the news outlets. We knew there were multiple US injuries and that at least two people were dead. There was also an ongoing hostage situation with the diplomats being held captive inside the embassy.

A rocket attack in the green zone around Baghdad was nothing new. There had been at least a dozen such attacks in the area, perpetrated by various groups. There was little doubt in the international community that these groups were supported by the Iranian government somehow. Good old plausible deniability again. Iran could claim this was nothing more than a group of insurgents trying to further destabilize the region.

As we sat around on the plane, we knew we had a few things in our favor. We had complete blueprints of the Embassy. We would know exactly where and how to breech it, with the captors hopefully unaware. There would also be the element of surprise. It was unlikely that they would be expecting an elite team of US military to be on site so quickly.

Embassies always had their own police-type force to keep them safe. The Diplomatic Security Service was certainly good at their jobs. They were absolute stars at threat assessment and predictive tactics but that did not seem to help them here.

While they were highly trained, they also had to operate differently than did we. In this case, however many dead bodies remained in the embassy when it was over didn't matter to us, provided none of them were US citizens or embassy workers. As always, our rules of engagement were a little different than any regular force.

Like most embassies, ours was also a conduit for intelligence gathered about the region. That was how the President, and his executive team were briefed each day. It was almost a joke really. Everyone knew that these embassies were staffed with at least a few military type people, in our case it was always CIA operatives. Unfortunately, in this situation, our information indicated that ALL the embassy staff were now being held hostage. There would be nobody free on the inside to help.

The number of people being held would make this challenging and the location would be difficult for us to get to. Thankfully the compound was large enough that we could parachute in. Our whole team would drop in three waves via HALO. The High part of the jump would be so high that we would be equipped with small oxygen tanks to keep us alive until we got into thicker, breathable air.

The plan was to send in two jumpers first to secure the area. We knew there would be guards outside but had no idea how many until overwatch got fully hooked up. The added benefit was that there was a tunnel that ran from a small room in the embassy, under the foundation. The tunnel ended at a location outside the walls. This would be the most likely method of extracting the hostages.

Many of our embassies has secretly added such escape tunnels. In more dangerous areas such as Ukraine, Baghdad, and others it was important to have multiple points of access and egress. The best ones were secret and untraceable.

There was an open field approximately 500 yards from the embassy walls and that was where our jumpers would land. Our goggles had GPS locators that were synched up to the overwatch team. A small red dot glowed where we needed to land with a lighter line showing the required trajectory.

The equipment was so sensitive and accurate that we could land on the deck of a small ship in rough seas if that was what the situation required. This was some serious nerd gear.

Iraq was surrounded by historically non-US friendly countries including Iran, Turkey, and Syria. The Saudis and Kuwait were a little more understanding of our needs. We were going to stage everything from Saudi Arabia.

Once we extracted the hostages, we would need to get close to Nasiriyah in the South before helos from Kuwait could provide cover.

While the Crown Prince of Saudi Arabia, Mohammad bin Salman, talked a tough game he appreciated what the US does for his country. At 34 he is the youngest Minister of Defense the Saudis have ever had. He is very progressive for that country. He ended the ban on female drivers, restricted the power of religious police and weakened that country's male-guardianship system. On the downside he is also suspected to have supported the torture of human rights activists and bombed Yemen.

He clearly wasn't a good guy, but he was the one we dealt with.

We were advised that we were headed to Camp Buehring, which gave us the closest access to Baghdad. This was one of the bases used to house US troops during Operations Desert Storm and Desert Shield. We could get in and out easily and it would not be a suspected location for us to launch from, thanks to the way bin Salman spoke about the US.

I awoke from a sound sleep to us landing at the base. While I was out, the XO and the Master Chief had nixed the parachute-in scenario. It was suddenly deemed to be too dangerous. That raised a few red flags for us, but we were often not privy to ALL information on these ops.

We were now going to drive from the base and stage ourselves, and the vehicles, around the open field. Changes in tactics often happened in this manner as overwatch and intel painted a more complete picture for the team.

We gathered up our equipment and went down the ramp of the aircraft. We loaded all our gear and ourselves into four heavily modified, large SUV's. Bullet proof glass, anti-IED structure, self repairing tires. These things had the works. They were not tanks but they were heavy duty vehicles that could withstand a certain amount of attack, and still move at decent speeds.

There were three Blackhawk helos on the tarmac along with a couple of Apaches. The Blackhawks were usually a transport type machine capable of carrying eleven fully equipped troops. This was the one you saw most in recent war movies. The two Boeing AH-64 Apache Guardians were a whole different story. The Apache is the worlds most lethal attack helicopter.

It can fire many Hellfire 2 missiles with laser tracking and has two 30 MM cannons along with other armaments. This one machine, piloted by two people, is capable of massive destruction in a matter of seconds. It also has significant defense mechanisms to keep it safe. The US learned a tough lesson when Extortion 17 was shot down so easily. We were also able to launch drones from this base which were extremely difficult to detect.

We sat in silence as we navigated the road towards Baghdad. Overwatch had been tracking the outside sentries at the embassy so it was confirmed we would stage in the field close by. That made it a substantially easier, although still dangerous, entry.

We would need to stagger the vehicles and hide them once the rest of us were in the tunnel and then return to pick everyone up.

We were on target sooner than expected and were making final preparations for the breech.

Fox 2 and little Bobby were going to be the first two in, along with Rusty. They would park almost a mile away from the field and traverse the balance on foot. Little Bobby, as you might guess, was far from little. What Magic had in height and overall sinewy muscle little Bobby had in pure strength. He was an absolute powerhouse while being at least six inches shorter than Fox 2.

The rest of us continued final preparations as the three of them sped ahead. It took a good long while to cover the almost 400 miles into Baghdad but soon we got the all-clear. We parked each vehicle in a different location, surrounding the field but still about a mile out. We split into two groups, Master Chief with half and Fox 2 with the other half.

We were all armed to the teeth, our sound-suppressed rifles at the ready. Each one of us carried multiple clips so, between us all, we had almost 2,000 rounds and that was without even counting the pistols. We had learned that if there was a firefight of any duration you quickly used up ammunition.

Firing wildly into a group was not how we were trained anyway, but one still had to stay on top of how much ammo you had. I also had my trusty garotte in my pocket. Like Amex says, I never leave home without it.

Chapter 40 – The Breech

We could see via GPS that we were close to the exit from the secret tunnel into the compound. We were going to move as a group to that entrance and then send four through the tunnel to confirm it was accessible. They would also assess the access points from within the embassy, that would enable us to better plan our attack.

We got to the disguised entrance without delay or running into anyone. It took very little time for the boys to cover the ground and soon we were communicating with them on the inside. The room that housed the tunnel entrance was concealed but had multiple access/ egress points. With overwatch guiding us as to how many bodies were where we would have pretty good eyes on the location. The power could also be cut remotely but that would be a last-ditch effort as hostage lives would be in even more danger if that was done.

Four of the team were left behind to ensure our safety once we started moving people out. When they were notified, we had everyone, and were moving through the tunnel, they would retrieve the SUV's and wait at the field.

We had trained so many times for situations just like this that we were perhaps more confident than usual. That confidence disappeared when two armed gunmen appeared out of an alley as we were parking our SUV. There was only Boone and I in this one, so we knew we had to act quickly and decisively. That was when Boone surprised the heck out of me.

He barked out something in Arabic at the men. I had no idea what he said but they lowered their weapons and said something back to him. When they got close, we each took one man and in seconds they were both on the ground.

Boone let Fox 1 know that we had encountered two armed men, they were neutralized, and we were on our way. We knew this would mean speeding things up. They could be sentries and we had no idea of their communication protocol. Boone grabbed a radio off one of them and tucked it into his jacket.

As we continued to move towards the rest of the team, I asked Boone what he said to those guys. He smiled and said that he told them we were IIS, also known as the Mukhabarat. They were officially the Department of General Intelligence in Iraq. The IIS was the most notorious and feared arm of the state security system. In reality, they were not all that different from Hitler's SS. A very bad group of guys.

Overwatch had detailed the locations of what were most likely guards and where the hostages were being held. These boneheads didn't realize that while grouping all the hostages together made it easier for them to guard them it also made it easier for people like us to get them out. There was always a worry of an IED booby trap on a door or guards left in the room, but our work was always dangerous.

You took it in stride and always did the best you could to use every tool available. There were now ten of us in the small area at the tunnel entrance. We opened the blueprints and marked the locations of heat signatures.

Overwatch advised that, based on their staffing information from the embassy, it looked like there were only two guards in the room with them.

We would need to attack silently and clear all the external hostage takers before moving to the room. Luckily, there was access into a washroom connected to the room where they were being held, directly from the tunnel room. Rusty and Boze were going to head to that room and wait for our instructions.

We could see on the blueprints where all the guards were, and we split into teams of two. By exiting through different locations, we were going to be able to come out both in front, and behind, the hostiles.

Rusty and Boze would take out their two first, giving the hostages time to get to the tunnel. Once that was done the rest of us would move quickly and almost simultaneously to take out the rest.

Once everyone was in position, Fox 1 gave the attack order. In seconds Rusty advised they had neutralized both hostiles with no hostages hurt. They were shaken up between their own ordeal and watching two heads explode right in front of their eyes, but they were all alive and safe.

The next ten seconds was just the sound of poof-poof-poof as slugs from our rifles found their marks. We did a sweep of the building and found no other bad guys and soon we were all moving down the tunnel. Even though all the hostiles were dead we had no idea who else might be outside.

The tunnel was still the safest way to get them out, although not the quickest.

The other four were positioning the SUV's and then it would be a matter of covering about two hundred miles as quickly as possible. Once past two hundred we would have helo cover and drones would be in the air. We would be as safe as we could be in such a situation.

We all moved quickly down through the tunnel. Thankfully all the hostages were mobile, and nobody was severely injured, just a few bumps and bruises. We had everyone and were being led by four of our team up front and four following up the rear. As we neared the end everyone held until those of us in front could ensure it was all clear. We exited the tunnel and surveyed the area while overwatch confirmed there was nobody else close by.

We moved across the field in small groups, escorting the hostages to different vehicles. We got everyone safely loaded and set off for Saudi Arabia. We motored quickly down the rough roads, operators surrounding the hostages. That way we had eyes out the back and both sides and with overwatch providing up-to-the-minute information we would know exactly what was happening.

We were getting close to the 200-mile mark when overwatch advised there were two fast moving vehicles approaching from the West. There was no reason to believe these would be anything friendly to our cause. Even with that, we did not want to risk civilian casualties.

Three of the vehicles continued up the road while we dropped back.

We hoped to end up behind the two vehicles, assuming they surfaced behind our three. If they came out in front that would present a different challenge.

We watched closely and listened as overwatch counted it down. We had our lights off and thankfully they came out in front of us. We could see the rear vehicle had some sort of large gun mounted in the box. It was likely a 50-calibre machine gun. The SUVs could withstand that for a certain amount of time, but it wasn't worth taking the chance. Those things were tough, but certainly not invincible!

We had an XR-50 with us that functioned and appeared like a standard rifle but fired a laser guided slug. The slug itself was also an incendiary device that would explode on impact. It was like a hand-held laser guided missile and was designed specifically for equipment destruction. You simply painted the target with the long-range laser sight, squeezed the trigger and off it went. Once locked in and fired the target could not escape.

I trained the sights of the XR on the vehicle with the gun and eased the trigger back sending the mini bomb on its way. A second later the rear vehicle went up in a massive fireball, so it was clearly the gas tank that was hit. The armor piercing shells weren't slowed by much.

One more squeeze of the trigger and the other vehicle was obliterated in similar manner. About five minutes after this encounter, overwatch advised the helos were close.

We were directed to pull off in a small clearing up ahead where we would be picked up.

Soon the quiet power of the Blackhawks could be heard and then they were on the ground, rotors turning slowly as we loaded everyone. They picked up all the hostages with four team members riding with each helo. We watched as the huge birds slipped quietly into the sky and headed toward Saudi Arabia at low altitude.

The rest of us had to get the SUV's back over the border so we put the pedal to the metal and got moving. Overwatch advised we could take it easy as there were drones in the air and they had a close eye on everything around us. There was no imminent threat, but we still didn't lay off the gas. Soon we were back in Saudi Arabia and within an hour we were all boarding an aircraft.

As we loaded, it suddenly dawned on me that our secret would soon be out. The hostages had seen me up close without my helmet as we rescued them. There was little sense in trying to hide it now, but I still went out of my way to steer clear of the embassy people and stick to our end of the plane. It was not usual to be on the same aircraft, so we tried to stay within our own group, buckling up into our seats and trying to sleep.

When we finally landed back on US soil, we just ignored the situation and hoped that nobody would mention it. I knew that wasn't the best approach, but it was all we had.

At least it would be impossible for anyone to track me down. SEAL teams operated behind a veil of secrecy and our identities were a tightly guarded secret. Other than a select few people, even our own military were kept in the dark.

As we walked away from the aircraft the Master Chief walked beside me and said it looked like the cat might be out of the bag. He would do his best to keep this out of the news. He just hoped that some headline-grabbing politician looking to make a statement didn't screw it up. We agreed that it could go either way. It could be either republican or democrat putting their own spin on this.

Politicians were shrewd that way. If it was in their own best interest, they would spin and lie about any situation to make it appear to either be their own or something they had nothing to do with. The angle they chose was only calculated after a deep assessment of public opinion. I hated the fact that MY achievement might be used as a feather in some politician's hat. It just wasn't right.

It was late, we were all tired and everyone just drifted off in their own direction after unloading at our cages. There were the usual high fives and good work from Fox 1 and 2, a little backslapping of our own and that was it.

This night the 93 miles home on the freeway seemed to take much longer than usual. I just had a lot of things running through my mind. Finally, I rolled into my garage and was in bed within minutes.

Chapter 40 One – Training

When I awoke in the morning, I had a text waiting telling me that training would commence on base in two days at 06:00. These guys just loved to get going early. Sometimes that really pissed me off. What would be wrong with a 9:00 AM start for a meeting occasionally. I supposed that simply wasn't a military thing. It absolutely was not a SEAL thing.

I was loving the challenge that being a SEAL was for me. Getting through all the training when so many fail was a big achievement. Staying on top like this was another kettle of fish. There were always people willing and able to step up and take your spot. I didn't feel like I had any special treatment being the first female SEAL, but I did put more pressure on myself than others seemed to. I still felt confident about my position and knew that I contributed to the team in some unique ways.

I think my varied martial arts skills were what made me almost the best at close quarters fighting. I also knew that my talent with a garotte and ability to get close enough to use that weapon was also a selling feature. In addition to those, I spent countless hours at the gun range honing my marksmanship. I was almost perfectly deadly with either hand using multiple pistols and my skills as a long and medium range sniper continued to improve.

Calmness was key to becoming a great sniper. I believe it was all the running that helped me to slow my heart rate very quickly, and then gently squeeze the trigger. That was often key to success as a SEAL sniper, sort of like the biathlon. Ski like crazy for 1, 2 or up to 5 kilometres and then settle as quickly as you can, control your breathing and be able to shoot very accurately.

I was already shooting at Chris Kyle range and wanted to get even better. I knew that three of the top five shot distances were held by Canadians.

I felt that with lots of practice I could get there too. It was unlikely to happen while a SEAL though because we were usually engaged as groups and long-range sniper work was typically a lone person. Still, I knew I was ready if and when I was called upon. At this point I truly felt like I was ready for anything and with my brothers-in-arms could be victorious in whatever was asked of us. It was a great feeling.

You just never experience that level of trust outside of the military. You knew that people would take bullets for you just as you would for them. It was like I went from three brothers at home to 13 brothers here.

I suppose firefighters are another group that think like this. Instead of dodging bullets and rockets they were being assaulted by fire.

A different type of threat but a threat to their lives for certain. Threats they knew they could eliminate as a team, each watching out for the other.

A couple days of runs and light workouts and some serious beach time and I was once again ready to work. Still, oh-six-hundred on that day snuck up on me. Late was never an option so all of us were at our cages preparing by 05:30. As we sat in the ready room the Master Chief said we had to work, and work hard, on honing our water skills.

He said we had to stay at our peak in that area. We all thought we were at our peak, but I think the cake-eaters wanted to be positive. There may be a specific mission in mind, or it might just be that we needed to be better than everyone else.

Even for SEALs, you were never quite sure what the motivation was.

When there was a specific mission about to be undertaken, we often trained using replicas of facilities or surrounding land. That training was different. There was an already mapped out end game in place and we were being timed and evaluated on effectiveness. That training was easy to spot as the Master Chief had us run multiple scenarios on the same end goal time after time. We always knew we HAD to be perfect or certainly as close to perfect as one can get. That was always what training was about, specific mission or not. Perfection.

We spent the next two weeks going at it very hard. Obstacle after obstacle we were being forced to change tactics based on fluid circumstances and without the benefit of overwatch. SEAL teams were always used in clandestine operations with the public, and even most of the military, not finding out until everything was over. We lived with knowledge only being given on an as-needed basis, so this was no different than always from that perspective.

Something DID feel different though and I couldn't figure out what it was. When me and the guys chatted at the end of the day a couple of them had the same feeling. It was nothing any of us could put our hands on though. I supposed that we would see in time if our gut feelings meant anything.

We were about three weeks in when Master Chief Kennedy said we should all take a couple of days to relax. He admitted he wasn't sure what was in the offing, but he hoped he would know this week. As soon as he did, we would be called back in so stay sharp.

As a SEAL, you are "sharp" all the time. In some cases that was a bit troubling. I don't think anyone on this team was currently in a PTSD situation but as an operator, your life is always in danger. That sets you up to live on a hair trigger and when you are out in civilian life that can present a challenge. Not so much the car backfiring and you drop to the ground type thing you might see on television, but much scarier scenarios.

Some guy might make the wrong move in a bar or somewhere else. Your instincts are instantaneous when you are trained the way we are. Imagine being the poor bastard who tried to sneak up behind a SEAL at an ATM and rob them. In my case, as with most of my brothers, it wouldn't make one bit of difference what kind of weapon they had. When the dust settled, they would be the one on the ground.

One of these circumstances popped up when me and Boone were grabbing a beer at a local bar. Not McP's because we wanted to be just two people having a drink. Just a couple of regular civilians enjoying an ice-cold beer on a warm San Diego day.

It seemed every day in San Diego was warm. People complained about it being cold when the temperature dipped WAY down to like 70 degrees and complained of heat whenever it topped 85. It was the perfect climate. Great for training too.

We were just relaxing when Boone bumped into a guy on his way back from the head. The guys' beer spilled down the front of his own shirt. It was innocent enough and Boone scrambled to say how sorry he was offering to buy the guy a new beer right away and apologizing for being so clumsy.

The guy had an issue for sure and Boone started to walk away when the guy told him to get on back to his Mexican Chica looking over at me. Boone made the mistake of laughing and said I was his sister, not his date. He thought that would de-escalate the situation, but it didn't. The guy then got all uppity and started walking towards me.

One of the worst things any military person can do is get into a fight with a civilian. All the training plus our keen sense of winning and staying alive makes for a potent combination. IF we did get into a skirmish with civilians, it was a guarantee that while we might win the battle, we would most definitely lose the war.

If the authorities arrived, it would be a double whammy. It wasn't like the old days when the civvie cops just turned you over to the MP's. Nowadays if it was civilians involved it made no difference who you were, you were off to jail for the night and perhaps charges to follow.

As he strode toward me giving his best tough guy impression, I stood to walk away still hoping to diffuse the situation. Unfortunately, for him, the bozo chose to grab my arm. As he pulled me back, I spun quickly, gained control of his arm, and twisted him face down onto the bar. I perhaps "placed" his face onto the bar top a little more firmly than I should. He was unable to move but I heard a commotion behind me and turned to see Boone mixing it up with two guys.

He was doing his best to talk them down, but it was not working. I told the guy to tell his buddies to lay off as I applied additional pressure to his arm.

He yelled at them to quit and the three of them just stood there looking at each other. The bartender and security still had not gotten to us yet, so I yelled out for everyone to calm down.

I told the guy I still had restrained that we should go out to the alley, so we didn't wreck anything and end up in jail. He said something like you stupid beaner, so I twisted even harder and then pushed him toward the door.

Now the five of us were in the alley squared off. I looked over at Boone and said I would take care of it and simultaneously delivered a kick to the head of the guy who started it all. He collapsed in a heap, and I looked at the other two and said we could either keep going and they could all get hurt or we could part ways here and now. They appeared to be thinking about it when the guy on the ground started to get up.

He was on one knee as I grabbed his collar and held my fist poised to knock him out.

I looked at them and said they had exactly two seconds to decide. The one guy said enough, enough so I just threw the loudmouth down and we walked away. As we discussed it on the way to the car, we concurred that we shouldn't have done that.

We also agreed that they most definitely started things and we tried to stop it. Nevertheless, we would be held at fault if this got out or got back to the Master Chief. I had long ago figured out that MC Art Kennedy was a rules kind of guy, at least from a SEAL perspective. The good news is we were out of uniform and in a bar not frequented by naval types. It was unlikely the story would have any legs.

We each jumped in our vehicles and got out of there in case there was anyone watching. I was ready to be finished with the whole night.

I didn't like the sense of unease I was left with and really hoped this would not go any further.

I was relieved to get into the house and up on that roof for one little nightcap. After a couple of sips and gazing up into the universe I was again calm. I had calmed down completely when my phone buzzed and there was a text from Fox 2. We were being spun up, need to meet at 06:00. Damn.

I went back into the house and crawled into my bed after a quick shower. I awoke, without benefit of an alarm at 04:30 hours. I got dressed, grabbed a coffee, and headed to the base.

Chapter 40 Two – The Source

We were all just shooting the breeze at our cages as we got our gear ready to go. We left as a group and were seated in the ready room early. A bunch of brass walked in with the Master Chief and Magic. We were all a little surprised to see the XO in that group.

With nothing but a blank screen behind him and everyone else leaning on his every word he began to speak in reverent tones. He said that many lives had been lost over the last couple of years. Civilians, military, our own SEALs. Whether in Afghanistan, Iraq, Syria, or other areas where the US was trying to help support democracy there had been far too many casualties.

He went on to explain that thanks to a huge effort from all branches of the military, the CIA, and other covert operators we now knew how they were getting their weapons. Automatic rifles, anti-tank mines, rocket propelled grenades and other sophisticated weaponry was being stolen and smuggled to these groups. The black market was a veritable cornucopia of devices designed to kill and they now had traced the trail of weapons and cash. There would be multiple teams in action, but our HVT was to be the ringleaders.

The XO said that we had proven ourselves. We were baptized by fire and confirmed in water. He had 100% confidence in our ability and now the rest of the squads would see that too. As I looked at the guys, new and old, I could see many were floored by the comments.

He looked at the group and simply said, Godspeed, and turned it over to ops to lay out the mission.

They said it would be a multi-pronged effort with simultaneous strikes in Iraq and Afghanistan. While we were certain that Iran was involved, at least passively, we needed to stay away from that area if we could. Our efforts would have three goals; eliminate the leaders, destroy as much of the tunnel infrastructure as possible and take out the stockpiles of weapons and ammunition.

While it could have been done easily and safely with drones and laser guided missiles and bombs there had to be boots on the ground to verify the result. It also had to be a covert operation. Using the teams meant that it could be a little more clandestine and would not necessarily have the stamp of the USA all over the mission.

We were told our targets had just moved into the Mosul area, a hotbed for insurgent activity. The ISIS fighters had constructed a massive tunnel infrastructure there.

It was used to hide weapons, people, transport weapons and transport drugs. Mosul was up close to the top of the country almost at the border with Turkey.

There are two US bases in Turkey housing nuclear weapons, mostly designed to deter Syria from doing anything crazy. Incirlik Air Base in Adana, Turkey was one of those. A mere 70 miles from the Syrian border it was an ideal deterrent location. For us it was also as close as we could get to Mosul. From there we would need different travel methods.

Getting in close would be a challenge but we would also have an advantage once we were close. We could use the Tigris river to both access the tunnels and escape once our work was complete. After all, frogmen are frogmen and we DO perform best in water. Once close to our target we would stage ourselves near the Al-Sadeer tourist complex. There were plenty of places to hide and hide in plain sight and nobody would really stand out in a location like that.

Soon we were at the base in Turkey and reviewing all details including confirming locations of our primary targets. I believed that getting in would be the easy part, getting out would be much more difficult.

We left in a blur of activity and made our way on back roads from Incirlik to an island in the Tigris river. I chuckled when I saw the name, Al-Jazeera Recreational Park. It was just across the river from the tourist complex.

We were soon traversing the river in blacked out zodiacs with extra-quiet electric motors. Rather than standard scuba gear we were using rebreathers so we could stay submerged for much longer periods and not release telltale large groups of bubbles. We landed on the empty side of the recreational park and stashed our boats. We swam safely across the river after a short hike through the park and met with our local contacts just outside the tourist complex.

Before we could get to the tunnels, we would need to cross under three bridges. Just past the third was a riverboat company the CIA had taken over. We would leave our boats there, gather a few additional weapons and then be on our way.

The operations were going to begin concurrently at sunset the following day. We got everything ready and stashed what we picked up in waterproof bags close to the riverbank. We could easily track them the next day with GPS. We reversed our travels and were soon back at our boats. We had small tents set up inside the bushes and it was just a matter of waiting for sundown now.

We took turns getting some sleep and then began final planning. We had to coordinate with overwatch and maintain GPS contact so we would know the details. We met as the sun set, loaded everything into our boats and took off down the Tigris. Each time we approached a bridge we would kill the motors and ride the current until safely past. There were very few people out in the late evenings around Mosul, so the trip was even easier than had been expected.

After no more than thirty minutes we had our boats hidden just off the river. We were directly West of Mosul and had to travel about four miles on foot before arriving at the tunnel entrance we needed to be at. It was a hub and spoke type setup with our two key targets usually occupying the middle. From that location there are eight tunnels radiating out and ultimately more than twenty spots from which to escape.

The key for us would be to get to the hub before being noticed and take them out. Once that was done, we could use RPG's and other explosive devices to destroy both those sections of tunnel. Destroying the stockpile of arms that was kept there would need to be timed to allow us to get outside the blast radius. A couple of explosive devices strategically placed would cause that whole area to blow. We had both timers and remotes so that we could set a timer, but if the situation dictated, we could detonate sooner using the remote.

It was far enough underground the shock of the blast would be mistaken for an earthquake. The ground above it would be shaking and rumbling as blast after blast melded into one. At roughly the same time, there would be similar blasts and assassinations going on in Basrah, Kabul, Jalalabad and a couple of other key locations known only to the XO and the teams directly involved.

This operation would not only take out the top men responsible for the deaths of too many American soldiers and Afghan civilians but also destroy their cache of weapons. It would be a crippling, and maybe even debilitating, blow to their cause. We were ready to do this, ready to avenge our brothers and all Americans. I felt exactly like I did on my mission to take out the killer who blew up Extortion 17, before I was an official SEAL.

Of course, on that operation I was solo. Here I would have my team, many others with the same goal. We knew we were going to virtually destroy an organization. This would have far reaching, positive effects, both in the region and back at home. Homeland Security was on top of everything that was happening on US soil. DHS had spies embedded with various groups connected to these operations. They had been tracking, recording, and monitoring all threats. They too would perform a massive sweep when our operations began.

It was unlikely the sweep would reach the news and even less likely that bodies would be found.

DHS had power and reach like no other department since 9/11. They could get almost anything done and the people being watched had no idea what was going on. There were very few search warrants and other legal obstacles to slow them down either.

Homeland Security had quickly morphed into an SS or Mossad type group, operating in the dark regions skirting the boundaries of the law. The main difference was, unless there was a proven threat, American citizens were off limits. They had information on everyone setting foot onto US soil, even those who had been there for years but were somehow connected to these groups. There were not a lot of AAR's (After Action Reviews) in the Department of Homeland Security. Often, it wasn't even a case of need to know. It was more like don't want to know. It was that simple.

Finally, the sun had set, and we began our move inland. We would much prefer not to run into any resistance, or anyone at all for that matter, but if we did, we were supremely prepared. Any resistance was to be met with deadly force. The only rule of engagement here was to complete our mission. Get in and get out with nobody left behind and leave destruction in our wake.

We knew we were capable of that and with the restrictions gone and the gloves off there was no force on the planet that could handle a SEAL team.

We had proven that repeatedly. The brotherhood was so strong, so focussed and so well equipped, at times we felt invincible. Of course, there had been tragedies involving SEALS and there were too many Ka-Bar knives with the names of fallen brave souls on them. It was one thing to FEEL invincible, a completely different thing to BE invincible. We knew it and that is what kept us on edge and constantly training and preparing.

Overwatch kept us posted on everything that was going on around us. Each team had its own little group watching over them. Fox 2 would raise his arm to stop us, and we would watch invisibly as a vehicle or two rolled past on the roadway. Overwatch was key to almost everything we did. They also kept fastidious records of all activities. However, unlike almost all SEAL operations, there would be no lasting ISR record on this mission.

The Intelligence, Surveillance, Reconnaissance (ISR) would all be real-time only. It would be used to track each team, guide it to its destination, monitor while engaged and then get us all safely back home. We were certain there would be things on there that should not be seen. It was simply safer to have no permanent record than to risk it ever getting to the wrong people.

In the hands of a left-wing politician such video record could quickly wipe out a government. While we were an apolitical group we were still affected by the politics of the day.

Finally, we were within 300 yards of one of the main entrances. We would approach straight on after their communication signals were jammed. There would be no discussion and no warning, each sentry was targeted by two of us to ensure they would all go down. There was a skinny alley between two buildings we would have to navigate.

We were certain there would be sentries up above, so we sent three of the team onto adjacent roofs. When Fox 1 gave the signal, we would all go into action. The ground team was spread out enabling us to cover deep into the alley as well as the front and sides. We heard a whisper that there were two on the roof and they were about to be handled. As soon as Rusty said they were neutralized, we took out the rest of the sentries and then drug them down the alley toward the cave entrance.

Thanks to ground penetrating radar, powerful satellites, and drones, we knew at this location we were less than one mile from the hub. Two other groups from our team had just executed the same actions at their locations. Although there were twenty or more exits, these three were the most likely to be used. Our team was moving through the tunnel first. We held at 100 yards out of the hub until all three teams were positioned.

These next 100 yards would be some of the most challenging yards we would ever cover. We would need to assess the locations and numbers of additional guards and take them out quickly and quietly. Each of us carried a modified .22-250 calibre rifle that was closer in size to a pistol than a rifle. It had two benefits. That calibre shot very flat and, due to the size and muzzle speed of the slug, wind had little effect on the trajectory.

Wind didn't matter down here though. Equipped with a very efficient silencer it was also the quietest gun there is. Inside of 100 yards, in the hands of a SEAL it was 100% deadly. All we heard in our earpieces was "go" and that was that. In mere seconds all men were down, and we could advance fifty yards closer to the hub, while watching very closely for any IED's or booby traps along the way.

Although we had all kinds of surveillance, the roof of the hub itself must have been lead-lined. We had no idea how many men were in there. When we got almost to the edge, each team would toss two flash bangs into the room. With special goggles it would turn into a shooting gallery. Before anything could happen though we had to ensure that the two key targets were there and covered by two shooters each. We did not want to have to chase anyone down any of these tunnels.

I spotted one and Boone spotted the other. We motioned to our partners, showing them which two they were. They were seated as calmly as a few guys around a Friday night poker game. There were no cards and drinks but that was the first thing that came to mind for me. The flash bangs were going to be tossed towards three of the openings where there were no frogmen. Simultaneously we would open up on them. As silence was no longer a concern, we could use our regular rifles, except for those of us taking out the HVT's.

It happened so quickly it was almost surreal. The flash bangs went off and you could see the slugs racing through the smoke towards their targets.

Our man was down immediately, two slugs entering his forehead and bouncing around inside his skull as they broke apart. He simply slumped forward in his seat at the same time as the other leader's head fell onto the table. In seconds, it was all over. We sent men down each of the other tunnels and were pleased to find them empty and unguarded.

We got some polaroids of the two leaders, drug all the bodies into the middle, and then started scouting for the weapons cache. We quickly found that section. There were hundreds of stolen RPG's, assorted ammunition, and other ordnance in crates. We pried open crate after crate, grabbing serial numbers from each box. Boze was wiring the whole area as we heard from another team that they had found a huge quantity of drugs.

There were bags and bags of what looked like cocaine and heroin all over the place. Gun runners and smugglers often used drugs to buy weapons. It was cheaper for the seller and the buyer could multiply his cash results by selling the drugs. In the underworld it was a win-win. Today would be a big lose-lose for them and their whole organization.

As charges were being set, we used their own RPGs to blow each of the other tunnels. It would seal them up from the inside preventing anyone from getting in or out. Containing the blast that way would also increase the initial assessment of the blast being an earthquake.

Once everything was wired and timers were set, we began our retreat, all of us moving back through the tunnel in which our team entered.

Soon we were at the entrance and our whole team was gathered in the alley keeping watch. We had carried out one last RPG launcher and one shell to seal this tunnel as well. They were long enough that the main hub would not be affected so Fox 2 took it about 50 yards in and discharged it.

He emerged from the entrance in a puff of smoke and that was it. We could blow it all right there, but the timers were all good and each was backed up with a second timer. We had time to get to the river and be in our boats when the blast occurred. That was much preferred by everyone.

After a double-time hike, we loaded our gear and launched the boats. Just past the first bridge we felt the tremors of a massive explosion that would obliterate everything in those tunnels along with the whole tunnel system. We opened the motors full out and raced up the river. It would be much safer for us to be back in vehicles navigating the harsh landscape than out in the open.

We got to the vehicles without incident and were soon bouncing along makeshift roads and trails. We were hyper-vigilant and would remain so until we returned to Turkish soil and finally back to Incirlik Air Base. It appeared that the massive blast would indeed be viewed as an earthquake.

The bad guys would know different but there were likely very few of those left. All that would remain would be foot soldiers, unable of crafting strategy or leading. The organization, for all intents and purposes, would be dead. At least for a few years anyway. It was a great feeling to realize what we had accomplished.

We were directed by overwatch to alter our route and, thanks to them, were back in Turkey minutes later. In stark contrast to how long it seemed to take us to arrive in Turkey, we were back in the good old U S of A in record time.

I will admit to absolutely passing out in my seat and sleeping a good portion of the trip though. I found that to be the normal case after a successful mission. I suppose being hyped up on adrenalin and living on the edge caught up with me and once an op was complete, I simply crashed.

We unloaded and took our gear back to our cages. Everyone was wiped out after this mission, and we simply scattered and went our own way.

Chapter 40 Three – Home Sweet Home

As usual I was excited to get back to my new home. As I parked and walked inside, I just took it all in. I thanked my aunt for her generosity as I looked over at the two now-empty brass books on the mantle. I knew I would never part with those and would eventually take them to my own grave.

Even though I had slept for quite a bit of the trip I still managed to bag a solid eight hours before waking. The next morning, I awoke to another perfect Newport Beach day and decided I would take at least two days off. No training, no sparring, no lifting. I felt like both my body and mind needed a break.

I took my time, enjoying a coffee and yogurt up on the roof. When I was good and ready, I got into some shorts and a top, put on some flip flops, and just started walking. I aimlessly strolled throughout the neighborhood on my way to the beach, admiring the many styles of homes here.

Like Venice Beach it was a real melting pot of architecture. You would find a smaller, brightly colored beach cottage next door to a massive, modern structure that looked more industrial than anything.

It was especially interesting to walk through this area at night. Many of the homes were quite large, covering almost the full lot. The massive floor to ceiling windows, especially in the newer modern houses, lit up brightly each evening.

People here didn't seem to care too much about window coverings either so as you walked you got framed glimpses into the lives of those around you. That is what made the nighttime walks so interesting. I would see a couple at a dinner table eating at ten o'clock at night and decide they were likely both Doctors. They had probably worked long, long hours and had together time whenever they could, after spending the day saving lives.

The next house and large picture window might contain a couple that looked straight out of the sixties. Living in one of the smaller, original beach houses in the area. The large, curved arches inside the home and ornate wood moldings made the room appear to be stuck in a time warp. Tie-died wall hangings and macramé plant hangers over top of oversized, pillow filled sofas. Completing the picture might be a grey haired, pony tailed older gentlemen. A true hippie I would guess.

Each house on each street seemed to tell a different story.

Soon, I had my own little piece of sand, and I was stretched out on an oversized towel. I would snooze off and on, music playing quietly in my ear buds. I really enjoyed the feel of the sun on my skin. It is so nice and warm and felt like a hug to me.

I loved my aunt for giving me the opportunity to have this for as long as I wished. I supposed that I might sell at some point, most likely move closer to Huntington Beach, but I was in no rush. As I drifted in and out of sleep, I even imagined living at Venice Beach.

I thought it might be cool to live on the canals but knew there was no way I could afford one of those. Even though my house was valued around 3 million, those places were in excess of five and ten million.

Then I realized how ridiculous I was being. I could live in the beautiful house I was in now with no worries about expenses for as long as I wanted. It was an almost perfect location and one I never dreamed of having. Why would I want more? Why would I want different? I chalked it up to good old greed and enough never being enough. I decided I would do my best to not think like that. I would enjoy everything that I had and share it with others as often as I could.

I dozed off again wondering what my next mission would be.
Other Books from C.C Chamberlane

SAVING UKRAINE – Megan and a couple of buddies save a few children and eliminate some Somali pirates before embarking on their greatest and most dangerous mission ever. Someone had to save Ukraine from its much larger and very dangerous neighbor. The Ukrainians were fighting bravely but Megan and her SEAL buddies would add a huge helping hand.

ABBADON – Megan Hernandez had become one of the most dangerous women on the planet. She was intelligent, tougher than nails and a deadly force when she wanted to me. Read about Megan's exploits after the government trained her as a navy SEAL.

SAMAELA – After taking care of her own demons in ABBADON, Megan directs her deadly skills at another scourge of the earth. The drug underworld had caused the death of one of her friends and now you can read about how she avenged that death. She singlehandedly wreaks havoc on the drug world.

Don't miss out!

Visit the website below and you can sign up to receive emails whenever C. C. Chamberlane publishes a new book. There's no charge and no obligation.

https://books2read.com/r/B-A-JWSR-QNUVB

BOOKS 2 READ

Connecting independent readers to independent writers.

Also by C. C. Chamberlane

Megan Hernandez
Samaela
The First Female Navy SEAL
Saving Ukraine

Standalone
Abbadon

About the Author

C.C.Chamberlane has been a novelist for a few years now. His first series of books include; ABBADON, SAMAELA, the First Female Navy SEAL and Saving Ukraine.

These stories focus on Megan Hernandez and her power and commitment to do good in the world.

www.ingramcontent.com/pod-product-compliance
Lightning Source LLC
Chambersburg PA
CBHW072349020726
47506CB00004B/1075